Praise for Killer's Diary

"An intense and compelling page-turner that will keep you guessing and engrossed from the first page to the novel's end... Those who enjoy psychological horror ala Thomas Harris' *Silence of the Lambs* will love *Killer's Diary*."
— Norman L. Rubenstein, *SHROUD: The Quarterly Journal of Dark Fiction and Art*

"A quick, entertaining romp that delivers on its promise."
— *Rue Morgue* magazine

"Four stars... the mind of a killer is delved into in great detail."
— Long and Short Reviews

"Quite simply, one of the best thriller guys you can find. No nonsense, no bloat, just thrill."
— Mort Castle, recipient of the Lifetime Achievement Award, Horror Writers Association

I0640300

KILLER'S DIARY

BRIAN PINKERTON

Special thanks to David Niall Wilson and David Dodd for bringing this book back in print to disturb a new generation of readers.

Chapter One

The first time he acted on the urge it was spectacular.

He wasn't sure what to expect, because most of the time his fantasies triumphed over reality. He owned a razor-sharp imagination, surround sound in high-definition 3-D, constructed by armies of laborers during his darkest years of solitude and suppression. It was a window, his getaway from a virtual cell. He scrambled eagerly into the arms of a fantasy world because he had nowhere else to go.

Like his earliest childhood aspirations of becoming a famous movie star, best-selling author, or jet fighter pilot, the acts of slaughter had begun as mind plays. In the beginning, there was no storyline, just a fast cut to the climax. He layered a dramatic symphonic score onto the sequence. The victims varied, but the adrenaline rush always pumped new life into his withered soul. Blame biology, genes, God or the devil, it felt good.

Those on the receiving end could be anonymous, blurred faces. Or they might be a particularly irritating individual who had crossed his path that day. Or perhaps someone repugnant from the TV screen. Usually they were women. There was something about their softness that invited the hard assault.

He did not value his own life, so he certainly felt no grief about ending another's. As a child, when he had killed a stray cat with an aluminum baseball bat, neighborhood girls cried. He merely found their reaction curious.

Part of the problem was that no one could identify with his pain. They lived in glistening shrink-wrap. They had not been beaten down into the dirt by those close to them. They did not wake up every morning with ugly scratching on the inside. A tireless heckler didn't occupy their brains, a cruel implant at birth.

He felt an obligation to share the hurt that ached in his bones. Once he wrote a poem called "Sponge," about a man who dutifully absorbed life's punishments, soaking them up until one day he was filled and could accept no more. Then he began squeezing out the vile residue, allowing it to dribble onto the ignorant people around him like acid rain. Their flesh melted away as they screamed, but the sponge kept squeezing until one day it was pure again.

Like squeezing a sponge, activating the mind plays helped expel some of the filth, but never enough. Then one day his inner voice picked at a sore spot and upped the antagonism. The Heckler grew more vocal with each passing day. He exposed the obvious in three short words.

It's…not…real.

The truth continued to taunt him, rendering his fantasies impotent. Neutered, the mind plays wobbled and crashed. A lighting rig fell to the stage. Scenery backdrops toppled. The audience exploded with laughter and scorn. The curtain tumbled down with a fast *whoomph*. Performers bailed. The dramatic tension had deteriorated into a limp burlesque comedy.

The auditorium emptied, the play closed, and his urges required a new outlet. Beckoning, the years of fantasy offered themselves as rehearsals for an electrifying performance on the world stage. Was he prepared?

Most of the time, he recognized the insanity of taking this show on the road, packing it up for a journey out of his head and into the light.

But he couldn't stop thinking about it. The notion swelled inside his cranium until the pressure was unbearable.

He shot into the neighborhood. He spent thirteen consecutive nights in various bars and clubs on Chicago's North Side looking for individuals who could fulfill his needs. He drank. He stared. He ran rigorous auditions in his mind, debating possibilities with the Heckler. He indulged in evil thoughts amid swarms of cheerful activity and enjoyed the incongruity like a private joke.

He aroused no suspicion. He was youthful and good looking. He fit in with the singles scene, even as he kept to himself and avoided conversations. When necessary, he smiled with warmth. He nodded. He listened.

He was a good listener because he wasn't much of a talker. He could go days without speaking, and then when he did speak—obligated perhaps by a store clerk or phone call he couldn't avoid—his voice croaked as if awakened from the dead. The sound of his own words jarred him back to reality.

At those moments he might lose his grounding. He might stumble. But he never fell.

On the thirteenth night of barhopping, he felt fully prepared, like a student who had studied exhaustively for a final exam. Any subsequent delay might dull his edge, weaken the momentum.

He identified his target.

Not beautiful, somewhat plain. Short, curly brown hair. Medium, nondescript build. Good teeth. Occasionally flirting with males, but mostly sticking to her small circle of girl companions. Drinking. One, two, three...seven drinks, divided between beers and cheap Jell-O shots. She took care of his checklist: unattached, losing some balance, speech sloppy, judgment impaired.

He knew the time was near when a bartender announced last call. She reached for her coat. Put it back down. Picked it up again. Teasing him? Finally she began snaking toward the exit for real, joined by her friends.

The Heckler ordered him to follow in a crackling radio voice, like a helicopter pilot viewing the scene from above. Tense violin strings lifted out of the bar noise.

His big scene had arrived.

Outside, in the sharp winter air, he pursued the group of girls, keeping a measured distance. One by one, individuals peeled from the group. He waited for her turn to break from the pack.

When she stopped to exchange hugs and wave goodbye, a prickling sensation traveled his body. One block later, when she cut through a dark parking lot, concealed from view by SUVs, he felt awed by the gift-wrapped location. He pulled on his wool ski mask, the anonymous face of death. He sped up, silent in white sneakers. Before his head could contemplate any new thoughts, the scene reached its glorious climax.

The four minutes matched his expectations closely, including the fierceness of the struggle and the wetness of the blood. It wasn't until the very end that something happened that his imagination had not prepared him for. It struck him like a slap.

Her eyes didn't shut. Crumpled to the pavement, still clutching at the stab wounds with tense fingers, she died staring back at him.

He had just removed the ski mask from his face. For a moment, he swooned and nearly lost his balance. The lights around him grew brighter and he heard distant noise.

In his mind plays, the victims had always closed their eyes, a final sign-off and departure. But her gaze locked on him. It took his breath away.

When he got home, he burned his clothes in the apartment building's incinerator. He showered and retired to bed.

He slept deeply.

When he awoke, close to noon, he waited for the crash of strong emotions. He didn't know when they would hit or what they would be. He just knew he had entered a new space.

His first sensation was hunger. He ate a bowl of cereal and drank some juice. He turned on the television and channel-surfed until he found his performance highlighted on a newscast. According to a solemn news anchor, the murder had taken place in the back parking lot of the victim's apartment building. A hefty Hispanic woman who worked for the Chicago Park District found the body kicked under her Jeep around seven that morning. With stuttering revulsion, she described finding the corpse and realizing that *the woman's eyes were gone.*

That's when the wall of feelings hit. He moved away from the television set. He paced a semicircle in his living room. He worked to identify the sensation. Not fear. Not grief. Not shame. Not relief. What was it? What was different compared to twenty-four hours ago? What drove the blood racing through his veins? *What was he feeling at this very minute?*

Alive.

Chapter Two

The first thing to catch her eye was the color red. She was sliding into the booth, purse flung ahead of her, left hand wrapped around a latte, when she glimpsed the spiral notebook with the red cover. It rested near the edge of the seat, where it had been hidden from view by the tabletop.

Somebody's already sitting here.

Ellen Gordon started to rise, then froze in a crouch. The other patrons had already claimed their seats. No one stood at the counter, where a young clerk introduced a fresh pan of muffins into the display case.

She sat back down.

Perhaps someone would come retrieve the notebook. If not, she'd deliver it to a clerk on her way out so it could be put in the lost and found, where it would join separated mittens and forgotten sunglasses. She imagined a DePaul college student searching his backpack for it between classes later that morning. She could even hear him cursing. *Damn it!*

Ellen popped the top on her coffee to accelerate the cooling. She checked her watch. Thirty minutes separated her from the beginning of another workday. She savored this slice of time—the buffer between home and work. It allowed her to enter the real world gradually before she had to face responsibilities. She could sit here alone with her thoughts as the morning opened up around her.

Ellen found comfort in the contrived coziness of Pacific Coast Coffee, an injection of Portland into the heart of Chicago. The interior resembled a mountain lodge getaway, with textured wood, low ceiling beams, a stone fireplace and hanging lanterns. While she rarely spoke to the regulars, they sometimes exchanged nods or quick smiles. Most of them were solo like her, fueling up on caffeine before heading to their destinations. Some were "grab and go," others sat for a spell to peel through the *Chicago Tribune*, *Sun-Times* or the weekly alternative paper, *The Reader*. Pacific Coast Coffee did not attract groups or chitchat. Interactivity was typically limited to Wi-Fi.

Occasionally, patrons of the bookstore where she worked spotted her. Their greetings usually jumped to the irony—the Book Shelf had its own café, yet here she was. Didn't she like her employer's coffee?

True, her co-workers indulged in the complimentary coffee, but Ellen felt awkward freeloading. Besides, she needed her caffeine sooner in the morning to carry her into work. Once inside the bookstore, she just wanted to do her job and hope that the hours moved quickly with minimal customer fuss.

Ellen took a cautious sip of her coffee. A jazz recording played from speakers overhead, fluid hands racing across a keyboard—energy without aggression. She liked it.

She checked her watch. Ten minutes left in the looming hourglass before she had to leave for work.

For a moment, Ellen's eyes locked on a display of take-home bags of coffee beans. The bags had an unusual color—pink.

Then she saw the sign that accompanied them. *What's not to love? Share your passion for flavor on Valentine's Day.*

The sign meant no harm, but it stung all the same. It was just like the cuddly Valentine's Day display at the bookstore, with thin, expensive books about love, sex and romance facing all directions. She had trained herself to avert her eyes from it. The display was a blunt reminder of the stone in the pit of her stomach.

Valentine's Day was Wednesday, all day long. She wondered how many people felt bad at this time of year? The hopelessly single, the divorced and widowed, the forgotten. And, really, how much true romance existed for the rest of them? *Happy Valentine's Day, honey, here's your card and flowers. We'll resume our cold indifference tomorrow.*

She checked her watch.

Almost time to go. The coffee had cooled to the point where she could take hearty swallows. She didn't smoke, barely drank, and had never tried illegal drugs. But coffee could be considered her addiction. She didn't know how she could face each day without the manufactured buzz. It brought her to life with a mask of enthusiasm. For a few hours, anyway, the things around her would matter.

She looked back at the red notebook on the seat next to her. It was plain and ordinary, the type found in any drugstore for a dollar…sitting there, alone and unattached, just like her.

"Maybe no one's coming for you," she said in a quiet voice.

She reached down and touched the notebook. Her thumb teased with an existing bend in a corner of the cover. She ran a finger along the thickness of the pages. They were not neatly aligned. There was a roughness that indicated they had been filled with activity.

She looked around the coffeehouse at various faces. No one looked back at her. Keeping the notebook on the seat, she opened it to a random page and glanced down. Just a peek…

Masculine handwriting. Sharp lines and angles, readable but not neat, rapid penmanship traveling the distance of every ruled line.

She read: *The last time I remember joy I was seven years old.*

Her eyes skipped ahead:

I am absent in my own life, a functional shell protecting a void.

She scanned the surrounding copy, not in any particular sequence, taking in clusters of sentences, the openings of paragraphs. She felt an unexpected rush.

Ellen realized she was reading somebody's private journal.

Sensitivity is my vulnerability. Pain is the reward.

She turned the pages. She locked into a lengthy passage. The voice simmered with free-flowing passion, captured in dark prose.

The people closest to me have hurt me in ways they will never know. The notion of consequences did not enter their conscience. In two years, I will be thirty, and I have surrendered hope that the storm clouds will dissipate.

Ellen thought, *he's my age.* She read: *I have no one close to turn to. No outlet. I feed my own sorrow. This journal will be a means to examine what brought me to this state. I will hold nothing back. I will spare no one.*

Ellen continued reading, fascinated by the intensity of the writing. The author alluded to traumatic experiences that had derailed him at a young age. The writing was candid and deeply personal. She read: *In these pages, I will attempt to undertake the greatest challenge of my life: to confront and dissect the unspeakable.*

With a loud bang, the entrance of the café swung open. Ellen immediately shut the notebook and removed her hand from it. She looked up. A tall, rugged man with a beard and glasses stepped into the coffeehouse.

Did it belong to him?

He walked over to the counter and fixed his eyes on the menu options listed on a sprawling blackboard in colored chalk.

"Espresso," he said. "Large."

The notebook remained unclaimed.

Ellen looked at the red cover. She looked at her watch.

I have to go.

Her boss, Terri Smith, rarely reprimanded her for being late. But there would be the glare, and that was enough.

Ellen slung her purse over her shoulder. She picked up her coffee and finished it. The final swallow was flat and bitter.

She studied the patrons around her. Preoccupied. She looked at the two girls behind the counter. They were talking about cross-country skiing in Minnesota. The rugged man who had ordered an espresso was busy at the half-and-half dispenser.

In a self-conscious effort to appear casual, Ellen reached down and picked up the notebook without looking at it.

It felt alive in her grasp. She felt frightened and guilty.

Was this like shoplifting?

I'm not stealing anything, she told herself. *I'll read it and bring it back.*

Ellen wanted to hear more from the notebook's intimate voice. It stirred and intrigued her. She couldn't abandon it now.

Ellen left the coffeehouse with the notebook tucked under her arm.

Chapter Three

When she thought about the notebook that sat under the seat in her car, in the parking lot, it gave her a small chill. She wanted to return to the handwritten confessions that were never intended for her eyes. Taking the notebook had been a bold act, and she was not a bold individual. Far from it—her former boyfriend, Jeremy, had called her "nonconfrontational". Her shyness and passivity used to drive him crazy. He would provoke Ellen just to get a rise out of her. "You're lifeless," he once told her, exasperated.

It's the opposite, she had wanted to respond. *I feel everything too strongly. I need to hold back.*

Jeremy hated how she sometimes flinched when he reached for her. She told him it wasn't personal. She needed time to warm up before becoming intimate. She wanted him to advance slowly, like wading into a pool of water. She couldn't be rushed. She locked up. It wasn't a choice.

Ultimately, her vulnerability brought out a meanness in him. She realized she was giving him a strange power; worse, he was enjoying it. That was when the relationship became ugly. His behavior triggered old insecurities, sending her back to the scared child she had tried to shed. A nasty cycle kicked back to life: she became desperate for acceptance, then defenseless under attack.

When Jeremy finally broke off the engagement, she was both shattered and relieved. She had no one to love her but no one to hurt her. She learned to embrace the loneliness.

The Book Shelf drew a small attendance as snow flurries littered the sky, keeping the casual crowd at bay. The people who did show up lingered, in no hurry to go back out beneath the sagging clouds. Many patrons searched for Valentine's Day gifts. She watched a cute little old man who never removed his earmuffs. He settled on a book called *101 Ways That I Love You*. Ellen was touched by the long time it took him to find the right book. He sampled at least a dozen alternatives before making his choice. In contrast, she saw many other customers make random, impatient grabs.

To fill the hours, Ellen indulged in an old game. She wandered empty aisles, half-closed her eyes and reached out for the first book that grazed her fingertips, pulling it out and opening it somewhere in the middle.

Then she read a page or two, without any preconceptions or advance knowledge of the text.

Sometimes she didn't know if she was reading fiction or nonfiction. She didn't know the topic or purpose of the book.

She only sampled the voice, eavesdropping.

She walked across the store, dipping into about a dozen books, effectively killing time. However, none of the books today captured her interest. They all seemed flat and dull.

And that got her thinking again about the notebook.

She had sampled it in a similar manner—not knowing anything about its author or subject. And it had seized her attention and produced tingles of excitement.

What made it so special?

She knew the answer. The notebook differed from the written works around her in a fundamental way:

It was never intended for outside eyes.

The writing was real, not manufactured for a publisher. The author was speaking from the heart to purge demons, not collect royalties. The words had not been edited by an editor, packaged by a marketer, self-censored by self-consciousness.

The notebook bled with human honesty.

———

That night, home in her apartment, bundled warm against the outside frost, curled on the couch, she held the notebook in her hands. The red cover was bland and generic, revealing nothing of the notebook's inner vitality. With an almost ceremonial reverence, she opened the cover to face the first page. The penmanship stared back at her, strong black strokes, urgent and earnest.

I am prepared to unravel my state of mind to isolate and confront the barriers to inner peace. The only way I can effectively accomplish this daunting task is through identifying and drafting on paper the elements of this equation. This notebook is my blackboard. This pen is my chalk. I am ready to see the calculation through to its absolute conclusion. Only then can I achieve the heightened awareness I require to begin the healing.

I am on my own. We are all chained to our individual histories. No one else is equipped to support my endeavor. No one can feel my pain. No one cares.

"I do," she said, surprising herself with the sound of her voice breaking the silence.

She read on. The writer journeyed deep into his childhood, collecting his earliest memories, identifying experiences that tore into him like high-voltage shocks. He spoke of losing his joy and innocence, stripped away like layers of skin, until he could no longer relate to others his age.

Cruelty and abuse are most destructive when inflicted on the young and unshaped. The efforts required to undo the damage far outweigh the short, easy jolts that deliver the first strike. The emotional devastation flows forward to predetermine the future. We are bound to the suffering of our formative years. The only hope is to grasp the razor wire with both hands and fight to free oneself, accepting the pain as barbed edges shred the flesh.

As the writer alluded to childhood experiences, Ellen's eyes blurred with tears. The stories rocked her back into places she couldn't avoid.

The two of them shared a common starting point.

———

For Ellen, the world had gone sour at age six, when her family cracked apart. She remembered the disintegration in a collection of moments, like a highlight reel: her mother sobbing at the kitchen table; the eerie emptiness of the house when her father no longer appeared at the end of the day with bellowing greetings and bear hugs; awkward phone conversations with her father after he moved out.

"I will always be your daddy," he tried to reassure her, a thin voice on a wire, nothing to hug. "Be strong," he said.

She kept the tears silent, but her words betrayed her, caught in her throat. "But when—when are you coming back?"

"Not for a while, hon," he responded, adding a heavy sigh. "I don't think your mother wants me to visit right now."

"Why not?"

"Well, that's mommy and daddy business."

He told her he was twenty minutes away, but he could have been calling from the other side of the world. Ellen pressed for a commitment to visit. She told him she had written new stories to share. She wanted him to give her more piano lessons.

"Soon, hon. Real soon."

In subsequent phone calls, his reply remained the same. He never offered a specific date or time, just "soon". That word kept her hanging for nearly a year before she realized he was just reciting reassurances with no real meaning behind them. She pestered her mother about her father's return, which did not generate pleasant reactions. Finally, her mother snapped at her in a brittle voice, "Why? Why do you want to see him? He left you, Ellen. He left both of us. He doesn't love us anymore. He's gone. Why should he come back? He moved far away and he's not coming back!"

Her mother's emotional state began a long slide. She turned to an assortment of pills to give her energy and to make her sleep. She began seeing imaginary bugs on the walls. She paced the house at strange hours. Sometimes, Ellen would wake up to find her mother hovering over her, staring and silent, like a floating ghost.

The money ran low and Ellen's mother searched for work. She accepted a job at the middle school cafeteria and earned a reputation as the "crazy lady who talks to herself". At school, the other children taunted Ellen about her "psycho mom". One boy, Billy Harth, was particularly mean-spirited and told her, "They're going to put your mom in a mental institution and then you'll have to live in the street."

Ellen continued to thrive on any contact with her father. In the early months, she received occasional phone calls and mailings—short notes or cards to say hello, accompanied by McDonald's coupons or small sheets of stickers. But the points of contact spread further apart until they only landed on holidays. Then he seemed to disappear altogether. She continued waiting for him. Every morning offered new possibilities. Every day concluded with aching disappointment. Eventually, Ellen accused her mother of blocking him from her, stealing letters and not sharing phone calls.

"That's what you believe?" said her mother, infuriated. "Fine. Then you answer the phone around here. You get the mail. You'll see."

Ellen accepted her mother's offer and soon regretted it. The truth became unavoidable. Ellen lost her enthusiasm for a ringing phone and the arrival of the mail. The pain settled in to stay. Her daddy didn't care about her anymore.

Eventually Ellen and her mother moved out of their Decatur, Illinois house. They relocated to an apartment building created from an old motel on a barren stretch of road on the edge of town. Her mother disposed of everything connected with the past, leaving piles of boxes on the curb in the splattering rain for neighborhood kids and junk seekers to sift through.

Ellen's mother sold the piano that Ellen's father had brought into the home for Ellen's fifth birthday. He was a skilled jazz pianist and had given Ellen weekly lessons. Sometimes they improvised duets with silly lyrics.

On a Saturday morning, Ellen watched from her bedroom window as another family took the piano away from the house: a delighted mother, father, two sons and a daughter. A complete family unit. She cried for the rest of the day.

As the schoolmates around her blossomed into maturity and independence, Ellen began her withdrawal from the real world. She spent increasing hours in her bedroom with the door closed, playing with imaginary friends and dreaming up stories for her dolls to enact around the furniture. She read countless books from the library.

Sometimes she observed the neighborhood children from her window. They ran in circles, laughing and chasing each other like strange creatures. Watching them caused her to ache inside.

The years following the divorce rocked with turbulence as Ellen's mother struggled to regain emotional stability. Over time, she seemed to be making progress. She left the school cafeteria for a new job, a clerical position at a real estate agency. She ventured out on dates. She spoke promisingly of finding a "new and better daddy".

But the man she settled for was rough, and he frightened Ellen. His name was George Ravenwood. He worked in a meat-packing plant and smelled like smoke and sweat.

George had a son from a previous marriage, a fumbling, overweight boy named Seymour, who was one year younger than Ellen. Ellen was encouraged to make friends with Seymour, but the two of them could barely manage a conversation. Ellen had a hard enough time making friends at school. If Seymour accompanied his father for a visit, he inevitably gravitated toward the television or brought a handheld video game. George often groused at the boy and knocked him around, smacking the back of his head with a cupped hand. The behavior scared Ellen.

Then one day, George's roughness extended to Ellen.

Ellen was watching cartoons after school, and George entered the room, tired and irritable. "I want the remote," he said.

"No, I'm watching this," replied Ellen, matter-of-fact. George grabbed her by the arm and threw her off the couch. She tumbled to the floor. Then he reached down and slapped her across the face—hard.

He stood over her. "I'm the adult, you're the child; you do what I tell you. Don't every say no to me again."

Ellen burst into tears, her cheek hot and stinging. "You didn't have to hit me. I'm telling my mom."

George thrust his face at her, ruddy and wide-eyed. Unshaven whiskers covered his cheeks like dirt. "If you tell your mother, I'll smash you so hard you'll think you got run over by a truck."

Ellen never told her mother. Weeks later, when her mother declared that she hoped to one day marry George, Ellen offered no reaction, which prompted a sharp response: "Nothing makes you happy."

George's visits to the cramped apartment grew more frequent. He never proposed to Ellen's mother, but he did act like the head of the household, barking orders, filling the big chair in front of the TV and taking control of the family finances. Ellen believed she was safe as long as she stayed hidden in her bedroom. She was wrong.

Ellen discovered that she remained in George's sights. When she reached puberty, his behavior turned strangely sweet, an ominous prelude to the horror to come. In the darkest corners of the night, he abused her. The first occasion was on a Saturday night, while her mother dozed in a drunken stupor. George, also inebriated, entered Ellen's room and made her do things that she knew were wrong.

He insisted that it was "fun play" that would bring them closer. He told her not to tell anyone. He said if she revealed their secret games to her mother, he would kill them both one night while they slept.

The late-night encounters continued into Ellen's middle teens, invading her slumber like surreal, close-up nightmares. She could not discuss the horrible acts with anyone. Instead, a swelling pressure spread inside her, turning her body numb.

To survive, she shut herself down.

The voice in the red notebook shared in Ellen's pain and delivered solace.

Buried in the words, Ellen found a passage that described her own feelings with such penetrating precision that it brought tears to her eyes.

As a child, I felt so alone that I carried my loneliness like a heavy stone around my neck, which caused my head to hang and kept my eyes trained on the ground. I felt consumed by some flu that I could not shake and no one could understand. I felt different and isolated, one of God's mistakes.

I learned to accept the pain. I surmised that somehow, some way, I deserved it. I no longer questioned my fate. It became the natural order of the universe.

The author alluded to a horrible, life-changing event at age seven, but offered no details. Instead he addressed the aftermath. He talked of losing memories to a black hole and awakening in the home of a senile grandmother in a faraway, nameless town, like a dream.

Ellen read from the journal: *My grandmother lived in a dark, static world of four rooms in a small square house on a dead-end street. Groceries were delivered. Curtains were shut. Cats defecated around us. I wanted to wake up from this strange, sudden change of scenery, but it was my new reality. I never saw my parents again. The box surrounding me shut and I lost the light.*

Ellen closed her eyes. It was almost midnight. Her emotions were on overload. She moved off the couch, revived the circulation in her legs and put the journal away. She prepared for bed, her thoughts still spinning in the past, pushed there by the notebook's bold tones.

Like the troubled author, Ellen had left home at an early age, but the circumstances differed. The journal's narrator had left home at age seven, still a young child, while Ellen had moved out at sixteen, straining for adulthood. Most importantly, Ellen's departure was a landmark of liberation, not suffocation.

She remembered it clearly, the day she had broken out of her own box with uncommon courage and discovered the light.

Chapter Four

On Thanksgiving Day, at age sixteen, Ellen planned her escape.

She began the holiday with the same sense of dread that squeezed her stomach into a ball anytime she gathered in the same room with George, her mother and Seymour in an effort to engage in a traditional family activity. She could still remember real Thanksgivings with her real dad. She longed for the genuine warmth of those days.

Instead, she now sat through monumentally unpleasant spectacles dominated by a puffy-faced, alcohol-drenched deviant who bickered and shouted his way through the day, pushing people around like twigs to be trampled.

When it came to George Ravenwood, Ellen had turned avoidance into an art. She slipped out the door to the library or went on long walks. But for something like Christmas or a birthday, her mother insisted on a full production that brought them all together.

To make matters worse, on this particular Thanksgiving the meal took place at George's house. George and Seymour lived in a cluttered split-level home that breathed bad odors. It sat next to an intersection glorified by a shut-down gas station, a convenience mart popular for liquor and lottery tickets and the blackened shell of a burned-down hamburger stand.

George supervised the turkey, which he grilled outdoors, standing in the leaves in his stocking feet. Hovering over the propane grill with a succession of beers, he lifted the lid every five minutes to both monitor and impede the progress by allowing heat to escape.

At least it was less ludicrous than the prior Thanksgiving, when he had tried to jam a turkey into her mother's microwave oven.

Seymour watched sitcom reruns in the family room, while Ellen and her mother worked in the kitchen on the side dishes. The meal was low-budget but well-intended, with green bean casserole, candied yams with miniature marshmallows, cranberry sauce from a can, warm rolls, sticky mashed potatoes and store-bought pumpkin pie.

As they prepared the food, Ellen thought about her father. What was he doing at this very minute? Was he reflecting on earlier times, recalling special memories of his daughter? Did he regret leaving? Would he phone and leave his voice on the answering machine?

Would he realize how long it had been since the two of them had spoken, and perhaps set up an afternoon out, maybe lunch together, maybe some Christmas shopping...

Ellen's mother derailed Ellen's train of thought with a loud clearing of her throat, followed by the comment, "Maybe today's the day, El. You know what I mean?"

Ellen finished cutting the carrots for the salad, looked at her mother and shook her head. "No. What?"

"George will propose. Maybe he has a ring. I saw them on sale at the mall. Thanksgiving is the perfect time, we're all together..."

Ellen couldn't help it: she made a sour expression.

Her mother slammed down the bowl she held. "What's that face for?"

"Nothing," said Ellen.

"You have no respect for him or my feelings," her mother said, reaching for her wine glass and taking a drink.

"I'm sorry, Mom," said Ellen in a flat tone.

Her mother moved over to the carrots. "I'll finish this. Why don't you just go. Go talk to Seymour. He's all by himself in there, go keep him company. Be like family."

Ellen left the kitchen.

Seymour sat on the couch, eyes shut and asleep, hugging a small pillow on top of his protruding belly. The laugh track of *Gilligan's Island* appeared to be directed at him.

Ellen seated herself on the far side of the sofa. Seymour opened his eyes and sat up, but said nothing.

She looked around the room—everything had been stacked in piles in a feeble attempt to clean up. One random pile mixed newspapers, clothes, a board game and a box of crackers.

She spied fingernail clippings on the coffee table. Or were they toenail clippings? She almost gagged. She fixed her eyes on the television.

"You can change the channel, if you want," muttered Seymour.

"No, it's okay," said Ellen.

And that was the extent of their conversation.

When the meal was ready, George called everyone to the dinner table with a loud shout. "Get in here! We're eating *now!*"

Ellen's mother asked Ellen to say grace. As Seymour chomped into a roll, Ellen murmured, "Thank you, God, for blessing us with this special day. Amen." She smirked at the irony in her words.

Ellen's mother and George consumed wine until they could barely get a firm grasp on their glasses. Predictably, George's tone grew harder and more belligerent, while Ellen's mother became glassy-eyed and clingy.

When Seymour attempted to pour himself some wine, George barked at him about being only fifteen. "So what?" said Seymour. "You let me drink all the time. You just don't want me to drink *your* wine."

An argument ensued, resulting in George spewing insults, most of them centered on Seymour's weight, which made his ears burn red.

"Fine," said George. "Drink all the wine you want, but you're not getting pie. You're too fucking fat. Look at you, you're exploding out of your goddamn clothes."

Seymour left the table. On his way out of the room, he flipped his middle finger at his father. George didn't see it, which was a relief to Ellen because she knew that any escalation would get physical.

George looked squarely at Ellen. "Don't you think he's fat? He's gotta be the fattest kid in the high school."

Ellen shrugged.

"Not like you," said George and his eyes locked on her. "You're thin, you have a nice figure."

Ellen felt a chill and folded her arms over her breasts. She sensed arousal behind George's gaze and lost her appetite.

After drinking another glass of wine, George began leaning into Ellen's mother, pawing her, while still glancing at Ellen—as if the daughter became the source of excitement for manhandling the mother.

When George's hand slipped under her mother's skirt, Ellen jumped up from the table and said, "Excuse me."

"Go play with Seymour," suggested Ellen's mother in a slurred voice, as if Ellen and Seymour were six years old.

The last image she took in was George's tongue licking the side of her mother's neck.

Ellen moved to the family room, where the television played without an audience. She paced for a moment, anxious.

When she heard George grunt and her mother moan, she knew she had to get out of the house.

Ellen grabbed her coat and exited through the back door. She stepped onto a small, chilly patio. Seymour sat on a picnic table bench. He looked up, startled, a hand cupped over his mouth.

He brought the hand down, revealing a joint.

"Hi," said Ellen.

"Hey," said Seymour. He exhaled slowly.

"Okay if I sit out here with you?" she asked.

"Sure."

She sat on the other side of the picnic table. Leaves skipped across the ground, occasionally mingling with garbage: a fast-food wrapper, a crushed Budweiser can.

She didn't expect conversation to follow, but Seymour surprised her with a low, rambling monologue.

"He's a piece of shit," Seymour said. "He used to be normal, when he was sober. Then my mom left him. She married his best friend. Everything went to hell after that. My dad had a good job, but he got fired, and now he's got a shit job. He just got angry and stayed angry. You best stay away from him. I brought a girl here once. He hit on her while I was out of the house. I see how he looks at you."

She said nothing, turning her eyes to the ground.

Seymour took a long pull on the joint, held his breath with a hard face, then let it go as his eyelids drooped.

"I'm leaving next week," he said.

Ellen looked at him. "What?"

"Getting out," he said. "Would *you* stay here?"

She shook her head.

"My buddy is going to Chicago," he said. "He's going to pick me up at school and away we go. I'm never coming back." He took another hit off the joint and then said, "Freedom," smiling at the taste of the word as it rolled off his lips.

Ellen rarely blurted out anything, preparing and thinking through every remark, but in this instance, she surprised herself with the impulsiveness of her words:

"Let me go with you."

Seymour shifted his weight and looked at her.

"Please," she said. "Just let me ride to Chicago with you. You can kick me out when we get there. I can't stay here any longer, either." Then the tears surfaced, wet and cold on her cheeks. "I have to get out. I'm going out of my mind. I need to leave home or I'm going to go crazy."

Seymour studied her. "Can I trust you?"

"Who am I going to tell?"

He shrugged. "You hardly talk as it is."

"Please."

Seymour grew silent. After a few minutes, Ellen feared he would not reply.

Then he spoke.

"Okay," Seymour said. And Ellen's escape was set into motion.

———

Each morning, as she prepared for school, she stuffed some clothes and personal items into her backpack. Once, as Ellen headed out the door, her mother noted the bulging backpack and said, "A lot of homework, huh?"

In gradual installments, Ellen accumulated the belongings in her locker, fearing suspicious looks from her peers, but no one seemed to take notice.

On the day of her escape, December 4, she brought two large trash bags to school. At precisely eleven a.m., she excused herself from algebra class, stating that she felt dizzy and needed to see the nurse. Heart pounding, she headed for her locker.

She filled the plastic bags with clothes and toiletries for her move to Chicago.

Mr. Murphy, her chemistry teacher, walked past as she was emptying her locker. She froze in terror, but he kept going.

Sometimes it pays to be invisible, she thought.

No one's going to miss me, that's for sure. The quiet girl in the back row with nothing to contribute, no friends, no life...

Ellen met Seymour in front of the school. "Jesus," he muttered, watching her drag the bulging plastic bags.

"Where are your things?" she asked.

"We're going to pick them up on the way," he said. His eyes darted nervously. Seymour had a reputation for trouble at the high school — ditching classes, acts of vandalism. Lurking outside school with Ellen, Miss Goody-Two- Shoes, while class was in session would surely draw attention.

Fifteen minutes late, a red Saturn pulled up to the curb. The driver was a scruffy, bearded man in his twenties with bloodshot eyes and a black baseball cap.

"Open the trunk," said Seymour.

As they shoved Ellen's bags inside, a voice erupted from nearby. "Hey! Ravenwood!"

Ellen turned. It was Mr. Daniels, the assistant principal. He walked toward them, squinting.

"Is that...Ellen Gordon?" he said, in a tone of surprise.

"Get in!" shouted Seymour, shutting himself in the front seat. Ellen jumped into the backseat. The car took off before she had a chance to close the door. The tires squealed from the curb. She slammed the door with a mighty pull.

Mr. Daniels stepped into the street, then stopped, hands on hips.

Ellen watched him get smaller and smaller in the back window.

She giggled.

The Saturn blew through a red light. A delivery truck slammed on its brakes, missing them by a few feet.

"Fucking Christ," muttered Seymour.

"What's your name?" asked the driver. Ellen saw his eyes looking at her in the rearview mirror. They twitched, creating a strange rippling across his face.

"Ellen," she said.

"I'm Randy. But you can call me Racer."

"Hello…Racer."

Seymour opened his window. He unzipped his backpack and started tossing out his school books and supplies. "Good-fucking-bye," he said.

Ellen watched through the back window as a trail of books, pens and pencils bounced on the pavement behind them. A blue binder struck the street, split open and sent a flurry of white pages into the wind.

"Freedom," said Seymour.

The Saturn pulled up in front of George's house. Just the sight of it gave Ellen the creeps. Seymour jumped out. He retrieved a full suitcase hidden behind a bush and stuffed it in the trunk. Within two minutes, they were back on the road, accelerating toward the highway.

Ellen had rarely been out of Decatur. As they cut through a steady stream of unfamiliar towns, she felt exhilarated. Racer played hard rock on the car stereo, blasting it until her ears rang. She thought about George Ravenwood never being able to touch her again. She thought about her body shedding the history of his touch like an ugly, dead skin. She wanted to feel fresh again.

The trip from Decatur to Chicago covered two hundred miles, a dramatic shift from the "Soybean Capital of the World" to a major metropolis. Chicago's crisp skyline and beautiful lakefront took her breath away.

Racer drove past the downtown area and entered a crowded, rough-looking residential neighborhood. Traffic slowed and the sidewalks filled with pedestrians wrapped in winter coats. The Saturn pulled up to a narrow building with a flapping awning that read *Amber Hotel*.

"This is the place," said Seymour.

Racer helped them unload the trunk. He shook Ellen's hand, his face still twitching as if an invisible force pulled at it. "Nice to meet you, miss. Good luck."

"Where are you going?" she asked him.

Racer grimaced. "Best I not say."

After he drove off, Seymour explained, "He deals. He gets his supplies in the city, takes them back home, sells around town, in the school. Hell, he makes more money than my dad."

Ellen and Seymour settled into their hotel room, a plain, square space. Seymour quickly laid out the rules.

"Tomorrow, we'll go looking for our own places. We can't stay together. How are you on money?"

"I've got enough to get started," she said. In recent years, her father had started sending her cash gifts for Christmas and birthdays, a token and empty gesture to stay in touch. Ellen's mother, seeing the return address, expressed no interest in the content. She held the envelopes distastefully by the corner and tossed them on Ellen's bed. Ellen's money stash quietly accumulated without her mother's knowledge.

"You sure?" said Seymour. "Because before I left, I ripped off the old bastard. He had a secret hiding place that wasn't so secret."

Seymour pulled out his wallet—it was fat with cash.

"No," said Ellen. "But thank you." She didn't want to touch bills that had once touched George's hands. She wanted absolutely nothing to do with George ever again.

The first night in the hotel was the worst. She couldn't sleep. The noises of the city—why the constant sirens?—kept her up. Her thoughts whirled.

Was this a bad impulsive decision? Who was going to take care of her? Where was she going to live? What was she going to do for employment?

She slept in the king-sized bed with Seymour, wearing more layers than she had on during the day. She was careful not to accidentally touch him, and he kept a distance from her, despite his bulk. But now, as he snored, she secretly wanted to move toward him and hold him, like a big security blanket. She needed her arms around *something*.

She was scared.

She thought about her mother. What was she thinking about at this moment? Ellen had left her a short note. She didn't want her mother to worry. She wasn't out to punish her. She just wanted to be free. The thought of her mother alone, the victim of another abandonment, filled her with guilt.

Ellen barely slept at all that night.

The next morning, Seymour woke early, muttered about finding an apartment, and left before Ellen had even sat up.

Well, so much for having breakfast together, thought Ellen.

For two hours, she walked the busy neighborhood, without a real destination, soaking in the new surroundings. The amount of stimulus soon overwhelmed her, and she felt anxiety throb in her chest and arms.

Ellen noticed a sad-looking old woman, face lined with worry, leaning against a brick wall covered with gang graffiti. She couldn't tear her eyes away. The woman appeared lost and alone. The image haunted her. In that instant, Ellen felt she had to call her mother.

She found a pay phone at a diner.

Her mother picked up on the first ring.

"Where are you? Where are you?" she screamed.

"Mother, please—"

"I'm worried sick. I'm throwing up! I'm out of Valium. I'm losing it, Ellen."

"Don't worry about me. I'm fine."

"I thought you were kidnapped. I thought you were dead!"

"Mom, I left a note."

"Kidnappers could have made you write that."

"I'm not in any trouble. I just thought it was time to move out and be on my own."

"You belong in school."

"I'll be okay. You'll see."

"Where are you? You have to tell me. Please!"

Ellen sighed. "Chicago."

"Oh, God. Where in Chicago?"

"It doesn't matter."

"Chicago is not an answer! *Where are you, Ellen?*"

"A hotel."

"What hotel?"

"The Amber Hotel. But I'm not going to be there long, so don't come looking for me. It'll be a waste of gas."

"Come home."

"I can't." Ellen started to cry. She looked around and saw patrons of the diner staring at her. "I have to go."

"Ellen, you come home right now!"

"Goodbye, Mom." Ellen hung up. She hurried out of the diner and burst into tears on the sidewalk.

She returned to the hotel room.

Seymour sat on the bed, surrounded by newspapers and a map.

"There are a lot of possibilities," he said.

"What?" she said, still in a daze from the conversation with her mother.

"Apartments. Here." He shoved one of the sections at her.

She glanced at the cramped columns of small print.

He circled another listing with a pen. "We should have no problems finding apartments."

She pulled the pages toward her and started to read. She soon found several possibilities and planned to visit them the following day. Seymour studied the listings for a while longer, and then they broke for a fast-food lunch across the street. Returning to the room, Seymour turned on the television and found a channel showing old sitcom reruns.

She watched television with him, even though the programs didn't interest her in the least. After two hours, the lack of conversation felt awkward. During a commercial, she got up and paced the small room.

She spotted a wrinkled piece of paper—a certificate—in his open suitcase on the floor. Curious, she stepped closer to get a better look.

Seymour saw that she was checking it out. He moved off the bed, picked up the certificate and handed it to her.

"I won the spelling bee," he said.

She examined the piece of paper, and sure enough, it was an award for placing first in a school spelling contest.

"When did you do this?" she asked.

"Fifth grade," he said.

It was several years old. Why was he still carrying it around? She didn't know what to make of it and handed the certificate back to him. He took it and said, "My dad's always calling me stupid. Well, he's the idiot. He never won anything. I won a spelling bee. I was best in the class. I'm not stupid."

"I don't think you're stupid," she said.

"An idiot doesn't win a spelling bee," he said, and he placed the certificate back in his suitcase. She thought about all the times she had heard George belittle his son, criticizing his weight and intelligence.

"Don't listen to your dad," she said. "He's a jerk."

Seymour replied, "I know."

He returned to the bed. The commercial break had ended and his show was back on.

Ellen felt sorry for him.

————

Night fell early and cold. For dinner, she suggested a pizza place she had seen during her walk that morning. When Seymour said that he'd rather eat at Burger King again because it was closer, she offered to go pick up the pizza and bring it back. Seymour shrugged, his hands resting on his large belly, his eyes glued to the *Dick Van Dyke Show*. "Okay. Fine. Whatever."

She left to get the pizza. On her way back, as an extra treat, she picked up a bag of chocolate chip cookies at a small grocery store. She was preparing to cross the street to return to the hotel when she saw a familiar face that took her breath away. She dropped the sacks of food to the ground.

George Ravenwood emerged from the Amber Hotel, pulling Seymour by the collar. George looked positively ferocious. Seymour stumbled to keep up, trapped, frightened and red-faced. He dragged his suitcase alongside him.

Ellen choked, mortified. She realized all at once what had happened. Her mother had told George where they were. *Why did I tell her the name of the hotel? It's all my fault. Oh my God, why why why?*

She remained frozen, hoping they wouldn't see her.

George and Seymour entered George's Honda. Rust outlined the doors. The car took off, headlamps burning into the night, a boomerang back to Decatur.

Once the vehicle disappeared from view, Ellen hurried across the street. She entered the Amber Hotel. She had to get her things before anyone came looking for her next.

She went to the room and quickly collected her belongings.

As she packed, she saw several of Seymour's items scattered across the floor…a sock, a T-shirt. Then she noticed the spelling bee certificate.

During the abrupt exit, it must have fallen to the ground. She picked it up, looked it over, and felt overwhelmingly sad.

She put it with her things. She vowed to one day return it to him.

Ellen left the hotel. She didn't have a plan, a destination or anyone to help her.

She was really on her own now.

Ellen found her first apartment, a genuine dump but cheap, later that week. She made the deposit, swallowing back the separation anxiety that plagued her. She resisted calling her mother for several months. She jumped at her first job opportunity, waiting tables in a Greek restaurant.

Over the next few years, Ellen changed jobs on a regular basis, working as a bank teller and then as a pharmacy clerk, generally bouncing around where needed as the economy twisted and turned. She moved to Lakeview, a neighborhood on Chicago's North Side. She found a "garden unit" apartment, basically a converted portion of the basement on the other side of a wall from the laundry room and storage units. She installed a massive bookcase in her living room and packed it with books.

Ellen faced the world alone, hungry for approval and acceptance. More than anything, she craved an intimate relationship. On some days, her unanswered desires filled her with sadness.

On other days, she felt a glimmer of hope that her soul mate truly existed, somewhere in the world, simply awaiting discovery.

Chapter Five

Ellen returned to Pacific Coast Coffee earlier than normal with a mission. *Who is the author of this journal?*

She purchased a large latte and brought it to an empty table in the back, near the booth where she had discovered the notebook. Before sitting down, she repositioned her chair for a better view of the customers coming and going.

No lost-and-found notice had been posted on the community bulletin board. No one appeared to be looking for anything. But every person who entered the café became a new possibility. She strained to hear words between patrons and the young girls at the counter. She listened for an exchange to begin with "I left a notebook in here yesterday…"

She tried to imagine what the author must look like.

She knew he was in his late twenties; that much had been revealed early in the text. The handwriting and tone were decidedly male. But the notebook offered no other clues to his physical appearance.

Instead, she knew him on the inside. The brooding, sensitive voice that ached with the pain of a detached childhood. She empathized with his lonely search for a meaningful connection, his waves of insecurity.

The voice was so strong, she was convinced she could match it to a face if he appeared here in the flesh. She evaluated every male patron who came into the coffeehouse against the voice, but kept coming up empty. The initial candidates were not promising: a slick, older businessman in a suit and overcoat, graying hair, posture solid with confidence; a jovial, athletic young man in a colorful sweater who knew everyone around him by name; a father with a wedding ring and active toddler; a pair of students, full of chatter about the previous night's dorm party and "beer bongs"; and several more men in their forties, fifties and beyond. Also, a few young men with young women in tow, including a disheveled couple still luminous from an overnight romance.

When a possibility finally presented itself in the form of a handsome, quiet young man with warm eyes, she wondered if he was a likely match or if it was just wishful thinking on her part.

The young man had wavy black hair, narrow, silver-rimmed glasses, a nice build, and an introverted, gentle manner about him. He looked around the café for a moment before stepping up to the counter.

She strained to pick up his soft speech. She didn't hear anything about a notebook. He placed his order. He received his coffee and sat down at a table near her. She watched him.

She allowed herself a fantasy where she approached him, the notebook in her grasp, red and vibrant like a beating heart. She heard herself say, "Excuse me, did you lose a notebook? I found this yesterday and wanted to keep it safe for its owner."

"Yes, thank God," he would respond, jaw dropping, stuttering with gratitude. "I've been looking everywhere. I really appreciate this. You don't know how much this notebook means to me!"

He would invite her to join him at his table. She would confess to glancing at the contents. She would praise his writing ability. He would blush, flattered. They would get to know each other and discover common bonds. The encounter would blossom into a full-blooded romance over the course of a few days. They would be made for one another. And he would never hurt her, because he had great sensitivity and wisdom and understanding. He would be intense and passionate, like his writing…

"Suzanne!"

Ellen's spell was broken by the subject of her fantasy calling out to an attractive, lively blonde who entered the coffeehouse. He stood up from his table. The blonde picked up her pace to reach him. They joined in an embrace and quick kiss. The blonde sat down with him, displaying sparkling blue eyes, perfect skin and a big smile of straight teeth.

Snapped out of her daydream, Ellen checked her watch. She still had twenty more minutes to play this silly game until it was time to leave for the bookstore. Her coffee cup was empty and she had no reading material. She pretended to take sips from the empty cup to justify her lingering to those around her. As if anybody noticed or cared.

More patrons spilled into the café, creating a line. Everyone seemed to have the same expression: tired eyes fixed forward, waiting for an opening at the front counter.

A young man with a soft baby face and pre-shower morning hair received a cappuccino and danish and brought it with him to a small table. Ellen watched as he shook a backpack off his shoulders. He reached into one of the pockets and pulled out a long, narrow notebook, the type used by reporters or crime detectives on old TV shows. "Just the facts, ma'am…"

The young man settled into his seat and peeled through several sheets before finding a blank one. He removed the cap from his black felt pen and began writing. His pen moved across the page in swift, crisp strokes.

Ellen felt her heartbeat accelerate. She studied him.

He was an earnest-looking man. Ellen could sense a match between his appearance and the voice in the journal. He looked lost in his thoughts, oblivious to the environment around him, even when an infant at a nearby table shrieked with restless energy.

Ellen considered approaching him about the notebook she had found, but something inside her froze up. She lost her courage. She couldn't craft the proper introductory dialogue in her head.

"Excuse me, I took a notebook home yesterday…"

"Hello, I couldn't help noticing that you're writing…"

"I have somebody's journal in my car…"

"I'm sorry for intruding on your privacy, but I've been reading what you wrote…"

It all sounded so absurd.

She found herself staring at him for an extended period of time. He never looked up. She could examine him as long as she wanted.

She shocked herself by imagining him kissing her.

He wasn't attractive or unattractive. But he would treat her well. She could just sense it. She would curl up in his gentle, caring arms. He would speak to her with great sincerity and soul, and they would find shared comfort, leading to intimacy.

Good Lord, an inner voice interjected. *Knock it off.*

She was a little too good at crafting romantic fantasies, no doubt due to reading so much fiction over the years. Her make-believe narratives fell neatly in place like well-laid tracks.

Romantic reality was another story. She could not control the outcome or dictate the events. Her skinny good looks drew a fair number of first dates. Once they got to know her, however, there was a sharp fall-off period, with fewer second dates, then fewer still third dates, until she faced a slim and disappointing selection of long-term possibilities. She knew that her personality had suffered ugly bruising in her youth. She was unable to let her guard down and open up to get close to anyone. Men grew impatient and stopped calling, sending her deeper into herself.

The relationship that had lasted the longest, nearly culminating in marriage, was the one with Jeremy. At least in the beginning, he exhibited patience with her skittishness and emotional walls. In exchange, she gave him the sex he wanted, offering easy loyalties, feminine curves, and a receptiveness to his adolescent interests like comic books and martial arts movies. The lack of conflict in their relationship compensated for a lack of any real spark.

She couldn't pinpoint the exact moment he turned cruel, but months after the relationship ended, she landed on a motive: he wanted a way out of the engagement without being the one responsible for breaking it off. He was working to incite *her* to call it quits. And when she didn't respond accordingly, he turned up the mistreatment until she absorbed an almost absurd amount of abuse.

She took the abuse because she didn't want him to leave. The pain of abandonment would be worse than the pain of mistreatment.

Finally, one day, aggravated by a multitude of problems, many that didn't involve her at all, he struck her. She shrunk back, cried, and her passive reaction seemed to make him even madder.

The engagement ended that night. He ended it with a simple sentence: "We're not getting married." He never apologized for striking her. She never expected an apology. George had never expressed remorse for his abusive treatment of her, either.

Jeremy vanished that day as if he had already expected the relationship to terminate. She responded by withdrawing further from the world, preferring her collection of books to people, reading to human interaction. When the opportunity arose to work in a bookstore, she jumped at the chance. She now spent most of her hours working at the Book Shelf or reading books in her apartment, a simple and comfortable routine. She had been proceeding on this path just fine until the red journal entered her life, stunning her by stirring passions and feelings out of the numbness. It was the last thing she had expected.

Now she had to trace the journal to its owner to determine if perhaps someone did exist who could understand her, reach out and resuscitate her.

As she pondered the thought, the man with the baby face and reporter's notepad stood up. His chair screeched as it dragged backward across the floor.

Ellen watched him, quickly glancing away when their eyes met for an instant. His eyes were soft, gray.

He walked across the coffeehouse and into a small corridor that led to the washrooms. She watched him disappear and then looked toward his table.

The notepad remained.

Ellen knew she only had a few minutes to act if she wanted to steal a glance at the handwriting.

It's now or never.

She rose silently, trying not to generate any attention. She walked toward his table while checking the faces around her. No one looked at her.

She felt giddy with uncharacteristic courage. She rarely acted on impulse and typically put deep thought into any unusual action, analyzing every potential outcome. But there was no time for that.

Ellen reached down and flipped open the narrow reporter's notebook. Her heart pounded so hard that she felt a throbbing in her ears.

The handwriting did not match that in the red notebook in her possession. The penmanship was round, crisp, almost feminine. She limited her stare to a few seconds, then moved on, across the floor to the other side of the café, where there was a counter with napkins, spoons, stirrers and steel containers of milk and cream. She took a handful of napkins, as if that was her true intention, and returned to her seat.

The baby-faced man came out of the bathroom corridor a few minutes later. He returned to his table, and his forehead furrowed for a moment in confusion. Ellen realized she had opened his notebook but not closed it.

Ellen stared down into her empty coffee cup. She felt as though arrows danced around her head, pointing her out, shouting *guilty*.

She couldn't bring herself to look back at him.

"Excuse me."

Ellen jumped with a gasp and looked up.

An older man with a gray mustache stood before her. He asked if he could borrow one of the chairs at her table.

"Of course," said Ellen. She promptly stood.

"I don't need *your* chair," said the man. "Just the one you aren't using."

"I have to go anyway," she responded.

————

During her lunch break at the Book Shelf, Ellen left the store and climbed into her car, her breath visible in the cold winter air. She slammed the door shut. The vinyl seats were cold. Bundled in her down coat, scarf and winter gloves, Ellen reached under the seat. She pulled out the red notebook.

She opened it to her bookmark, a childhood gift from her father more than two decades ago, a slender blue strip with the words *Books Are Friends* printed in bold simplicity. She returned to the page where she had left off the night before.

She read for fifteen minutes, lost in every word as the prose became darker and bleaker, descending like steps into a private hell. She recognized her own darkest period of hopelessness and despair in a long passage that described the author's desire to end his life.

I find myself conjuring images of the many ways I could leave this world, witnessing the act and then lingering on the image of my body after my spirit has passed on, reducing my existence in this world to an empty vessel that cannot feel love, pain or even the dreariness of indifference. I crave this departure but I keep the feelings at bay. What saves me from acting on them is the determination that I will, I must rise above this spiritual crisis. I will be strong again. I will rediscover hope.

Whack! Whack!

A round, pink face appeared at the driver's side window, inches away from Ellen, accompanied by a loud rapping of knuckles.

"Hey!" said the face.

Ellen slapped the notebook shut. She dropped it into her lap and faced her co-worker Peg.

Peg's freckled face bobbed for a better view, curious and grinning. "What're you doing in there?" she asked. "Aren't you freezing? What're you reading?"

Chapter Six

He sat in his favorite chair facing the window that overlooked the busy street below, watching the activity through the glass like a large-screen television.

This television program even had a regular cast. There was Old Woman with Dog, faithfully picking up the droppings with a newspaper (*Chicago Sun-Times*). There was Rollerblade Girl, wearing pigtails to appear youthful but middle-aged when seen from the rear, chatting up the young men in the neighborhood. There was Mr. Cigarette Break, periodically stepping outside of the hair salon to steal five minutes of quick puffs.

And there was Oranjacket.

Aside from the orange jacket that covered a slight build, short black hair and big glasses, he knew exactly five things about this woman.

She worked at a little grocery store two blocks away.

She came home at approximately ten fifteen every night except Sunday, her day off.

She lived in the building across the street on the third floor.

He had once seen her naked pink legs and white panties before the blinds had fallen shut.

She lived alone.

Tonight Oranjacket did not fail him. At 10:17 p.m., she appeared on the sidewalk, alone, eyes fixed ahead, oblivious to the world around her, slumped somewhat, probably tired and possibly sad.

How many truly happy people are there?

She seemed inconsequential in the scattered after-hours crowd. As she entered the vestibule of her building, she disappeared from view and his mind play took over…

———

She checked her mail.

Bills, junk, perhaps a catalogue of nice things, the latest fashions to fantasize about in bed before drifting off to sleep, legs naked under the sheets.

As she shut her mail box, he appeared next to her. Casual, young and well-groomed. No cause for alarm. Not like one of those scary, foul homeless lumps who roamed the neighborhood. He could have been one of the graduate students at the nearby college.

He said a friendly hello to her and reached into his pocket. He took out a key chain, as if to check his own mailbox.

She said, ever so faint and shy, "Hi," and advanced to unlock the main door leading to the stairs. She entered the building's interior and did not look back.

He caught the door with the tips of his fingers just before it slammed and latched shut.

She moved up the steps in small, thunking footsteps. Keeping his own steps soundless, staying on the carpeted section of the stairs, he followed Oranjacket to her apartment.

She reached her door, unlocked it, entered the apartment and flicked on the lights—an automated sequence of events, which she had performed hundreds of times before. But this time something interrupted the routine. Something moved behind her. A dark shape.

Before she could turn for a better look, a strong force slammed into her from behind. She fell hard to the floor, wind knocked out of her. From an awkward angle—low, tilted—she saw a man wearing a ski mask over his face. He stepped inside her apartment. He shut the door and locked them in together.

As she struggled to return to her feet, he snapped off the lights. She gasped as he landed on her, his knee in her belly. He held her down with his left hand covering her face. The right hand gripped the handle on a four-inch hunting knife. He said, "Let me hear your death scream…"

———

Oranjacket shed her coat and placed it on a small sofa. She walked to the window, offering him a better look, briefly, before shutting the blinds.

In the moment that she faced outward, she had no expression on her face. She had no idea. She had no fucking idea.

Sitting in his favorite chair, looking through his window at her window, a screen within a screen, he continued to stare at the closed blinds, burning his gaze through them, through her clothes, through her flesh…

I did it before, I can do it again.

His first elimination from the human race, the girl in the parking lot, had been remarkably easy. It had been the first time in his life that he realized he wielded some power. He could hurt the world that damaged him. The role of victim and perpetrator had been reversed, and it had felt like fresh air in his lungs, a revelation. He could rise above the sludge below, the insect people, and manipulate them as he chose, one at a time.

As long as his efforts remained on a small scale, the world did not fight back. A fellow citizen had been removed, a stranger plucked from the land of the living, and aside from the momentary alarm of a headline, it was business as usual. No one cared unless it was their turn. Looking at the street below, the scene became evidence that this dense urban jungle just kept on going, even after losing one of its own. There was one less straggler on the sidewalk to navigate around. One less cast member in the world's playhouse.

Confidence hardened his muscles and bones. He could continue his work in this environment, sacrificing strangers to bring his own life back from the dead, draining the vitality out of them for his own rejuvenation.

A long time ago, a psychiatrist had told him he lacked goals. It was true. He had not identified any passions that would motivate him. He was adrift. But now he had a desired end-state. A go-forward strategy. He knew precisely what he wanted and the focus was clear.

He couldn't hurt the people who hurt him all those years ago. But he could pay it forward. His goal was to expel all of the pain inside him, delivering it to others, like a special mailman, until he became cleansed, a newborn without a trace of history, unchained from the past, the ultimate state of freedom.

Chapter Seven

A t eleven thirty p.m., well beyond her traditional bedtime, Ellen passed the halfway point in the red spiral notebook. She based the milestone on the thickness of the pages completed and the pages unread.

She felt a pang of sorrow. She had consumed more of the journal than remained unexplored.

Each night, she had read a generous portion, careful not to plow too quickly forward, savoring every page…while preserving enough to occupy subsequent nights.

She dreaded the day that her relationship with this voice would come to an end.

After the unexpected interruption from her co-worker Peg in the Book Shelf parking lot, Ellen had limited herself to only reading the journal at home.

Each night, after dinner, she lit a scented candle. She poured herself a glass of red wine. She curled on the couch with an old blanket knitted by her grandmother.

And she entered the innermost thoughts and passions of this intense and mysterious young man.

She joined him on a long journey through his brutal childhood, and while it awoke her own traumatic experiences, some unrecalled for many years, the sensations felt more comforting than painful. She found solace in their crossed paths, an escape route from the isolation of her own back history. She marveled over this stranger's ability to describe her emotions in his words.

She wished she could write about her own psychological wounds in such a revelatory manner, picking the perfect descriptions and analogies, letting the feelings flow, equal parts anger, eloquence and therapy. It was the release she needed. She had tried yoga, jogging, swimming, pottery, night classes and, yes, even heaps of caffeine, to feel better. Everything except facing her demons head on.

Reading this young man's private journal, she realized she had never felt so close to anyone before. Not Jeremy, and certainly not her family. She had never entered someone's inner world like this. Long after she put the notebook down, his brooding voice remained inside her. Sometimes his phrases stayed with her into the following day, rolling through her thoughts at the bookstore.

In the entries she read tonight, the author spoke about a troubled brother for the first time. His name was Darren, and he was younger. The passages displayed heartfelt sympathy—and concern—for a sibling who had endured much of the same pain during his upbringing, yet suffered far worse in the present day.

While the trauma of my youth has left me in a state of unrest and melancholy that troubles me into adulthood, I am able to find some solace in the fact that I have remained socially functional and outwardly decent, having escaped the depths of madness that still plague my brother Darren, wrote the author.

Last night, I awoke to thundering fists against my front door that could only belong to my panic-prone sibling. I could tell from the intensity of the blows that Darren had erupted into his highest levels of paranoia, fighting off the stranglehold of his demons with unfocused rage. I sat him in my kitchen and tried to contain and calm him, grateful that he had come to me and not gotten himself in trouble, a constant fear of mine when he sheds all rational behavior.

My brother has endured these fits for years, but rarely do they achieve a scale like this, where I worry about his safety.

He has abandoned his doctors and medication. I have become his only treatment. Fortunately he listens to me and understands...for now. We have a unique bond.

By early the next morning, he rediscovered his true self, and was ashamed by his loss of control. When he left my apartment, I felt confident that Darren was no longer a risk to himself or anyone else. What I could not know was the timing of his next fit or "seizure," as he calls them.

I have seen years pass between episodes, but I have also seen a gap of only a few days.

I understand his struggles in ways no one else can. As long as he knows to find me, I will be his stronger half. I am confident that Darren will not succumb to the darkness.

My brother is the only person I am truly close to. Perhaps one day I will find a female companion, someone to love with all my strength and heart. But I fear that my battle scars and heavy moods will be too much of a burden for even the most patient and tolerant young woman. I dare not undertake a search for this individual because I dread adding further disappointment to my life.

If she is out there, how will I know?

Now it was nearly midnight.

Ellen placed the journal in the top drawer of her computer desk. She was too worked up to sleep, so she decided to take a bath. She filled the tub, adding a dose of bubbles, unwrapping a new, sweet-smelling soap. She lit a scented candle on the sink counter and turned out the lights. She stepped naked from the chilled air into the steaming water's grip, sinking slowly, rolling to her back, bringing her head to a rest against a plastic pillow.

The candlelight flickered, dancing with its partner in the mirror.

Ellen closed her eyes.

She imagined what the writer must look like. She started with the eyes. Deep blue. Sensitive. Medium-length hair, dirty blond, untamed, wavy. A sleek and honed physique, broad shoulders, graceful hands. Thin lips.

She crafted his image, brought him into her bed and pulled him into her fantasies. Their passions were an equal match. He unwound her hair, let it flow, and stroked it with long fingers. Sturdy and caring, he embraced her into safety.

"I need you," he said…

Chapter Eight

When the alarm sounded, Ellen stopped it with a slap of resentment, having been yanked from one of her better dreams. Typically her dreams were grounded in insecurity or apprehension, amplifying moods she couldn't shake during the day. But this latest dream—

She sat up and had to laugh. It was a romance.

Ellen didn't ordinarily fantasize about men with such graphic intensity, awake or asleep. But this journal, through its vivid writing and brooding emotions, had manifested itself into a living, breathing human being. This being had stepped into her subconscious world, impossibly handsome and passionate. He had held her and kissed her lips, causing her to grow warm and prickly under the sheets. Sitting up in bed, she could smell the scent of her sweat and feel the beating of her heart.

The dream imagery began to dissolve, but she kept the fantasy alive, reminding herself that the journal and its voice were still very real.

She wanted to read another passage right then. Just a couple of paragraphs—maybe one page max. But she knew that once she got started, she wouldn't be able to stop. There was something better about saving the journal for that evening, a reward waiting at the end of the day, something to get her through the monotony of work. At night, under the cover of darkness, without distractions or obligations, she could re-enter the pages and lose herself in them, like a little girl exploring a forbidden forest.

Until then, she left the journal in the drawer of her computer desk, out of sight but a constant presence.

Ellen climbed off the bed. She disrobed and felt the fading tingles on her skin. She glanced at the clock on her way to the shower.

If she moved quickly, she would have at least one hour to spend in the coffeehouse, continuing her search for the journal's author.

———

Ellen returned to her post, a small table near the booth where she had discovered the notebook. She held a large latte and took measured sips. It was her second of two cups, intended to last thirty minutes each. She kept a newspaper spread out in front of her—a prop, because she wasn't reading.

She settled into her new routine. She watched the clientele as it turned over in small, continual waves. She recognized familiar faces and several individuals she had already ruled out. Many of the others could be considered candidates. She had a good handle on age and gender, but little else.

Glancing around the room, Ellen couldn't find anyone using a pen. Two men pecked at laptops, including a young, bald African-American in a business suit.

She wondered how long she would continue this activity— searching out the journal's author. Weeks? Months?

Perhaps it would be better if she never found him and let her fantasies take over completely. Reality could be a crushing disappointment. It usually was.

At quarter to nine, Ellen needed to head to work. She allowed herself three more minutes just in case, and didn't gain anything from it. She picked up her purse and decided to take a quick bathroom break before starting her shift at the Book Shelf.

In the bathroom mirror, Ellen gave herself a long look, something she rarely did.

She studied herself as if stealing a glance at someone else—just another patron in the coffeehouse—another face to review.

In that moment, detached, absent of all self-consciousness and brain baggage, she thought, *Hey, I'm kind of cute.*

She brushed her hair, straightened herself up, and even smiled.

The smile *really* looked like someone else.

She told herself, *Let's get through another day at work, watch the hours fly by, and then tonight, a little wine, pillows on the sofa and a deep dive back into the journal.*

She left the bathroom and began moving through the coffeehouse. She wasn't even looking at customers anymore. But then someone caught her eye. She noticed a hunched figure seated by the wall, occasionally blocked from view by moving patrons. This person was new: a young man wearing a black sweater, facing away from everybody, with long, dark locks of hair rolling down the back of his neck.

Did I not notice him before? Did he just arrive?

Ellen continued at her pace, but curved her path to get a closer look at the young man in the black sweater.

She needed a quick excuse for her detour and found it: the community bulletin board, covered with notices of local events, charity drives, and citizens offering specialized services like dog-walking and tarot card readings.

She faced the bulletin board with her head cocked, as if engaged. *Local Magician Available for Kids' Birthday Parties*! Ellen's gaze moved off the bulletin board. She looked to the far right to catch a glimpse...

The young man's head hung low. His arms rested on the table, circling an open notebook. Gripping a black pen, his hand moved across a page, making quick, decisive strokes.

Ellen had to turn her head to get a better look.

She needed to see the handwriting.

It remained out of view.

I need to get closer to him.

The young man's arms, his slumped frame, the position of the table—all of it kept his writing hidden.

Ellen felt a sudden urge to leave the coffeehouse. Anxiety buzzed in her chest and arms. She realized how awkward she must have appeared at that moment, frozen at the bulletin board, but not really looking at it.

Do something or leave! screamed an inner voice.

Ellen approached the young man. Heart pounding, she stood over him.

He looked up.

His face was solemn, eyes dark, ringed with fatigue, but soulful. He was handsome.

"Hi—" said Ellen. "Can I—borrow your pen?"

He opened his mouth to respond, but she continued: "I just need to write down a phone number…from the bulletin board…guitar lessons." She smiled, even forcing a little laugh.

"Okay," he said in a quiet voice. He rested his gaze on her, straightening his posture. He held out the pen to her.

She moved closer to accept it.

Her eyes shot downward. The notebook. The handwriting.

It's him. The handwriting was identical to that in the journal she had in her possession.

"Th-thanks," she said, stuttering on the one word. She took the pen from him, absorbing every detail of the moment, seeing a firm, masculine hand, dark hair swirling on the back of his wrist.

"No problem," he said.

When she remained frozen for an extra moment, he asked, "Do you need a piece of paper?"

She nodded. Of course she did. "Yes. That would be great. Thank you."

He reached down to the notebook and flipped ahead to a blank page. He took hold of a sheet and tore it free from the spiral binding.

With his attention on the notebook, she seized the extra seconds to study him all over, and he was beautiful. He had broad shoulders, light facial stubble, and an earthy—not slick—presence about him. The image matched her imagination. She dipped back into her prickly, floating dream state. The entire moment felt surreal.

"There you go," he said, handing her the piece of paper.

She accepted it, sputtering one more word of thanks. She quickly moved to the bulletin board.

She wondered if his eyes remained on her.

She studied the bulletin board, feeling as if the attention of the world were on her, dizzy from a strange blend of panic and exhilaration.

Where are those guitar lessons?

She found the notice and wrote the phone number down in careful, slow penmanship, like a child. She needed every extra moment to catch her breath and regroup.

I know the author of the notebook. Now what? What's the next step?

She decided there was no next step. This was all she needed for now. Meeting him was overwhelming enough. Her game plan was to return the pen, say thank you one more time and get out of the coffeehouse before she babbled something stupid or made him suspicious.

She stuffed the phone number into her purse. She returned to him, arm extended with the pen for a quick handoff, afraid to linger.

He let the pen dangle in the air for a moment before reaching for it. His eyes stayed on her.

She didn't know whether to look away or return the look.

He was staring.

"Wait a minute," he said. "I know you."

She said, "I don't think…"

But he continued, "You have something that belongs to me."

She just about shattered to pieces right then and there.

He knows I have the notebook.

She opened her mouth to begin the confession, but he spoke first.

"You work at the Book Shelf," he said. "You're holding a book for me there."

"I am?"

"Yes, I ordered it a couple of weeks ago. You took the order. The store just called to tell me that it came in."

She didn't remember him. But that was hardly unusual—hundreds of visitors came into the store every day. Most of the time, they blurred together into an anonymous blob, unless a complaint or extended encounter distinguished them. Her shyness usually resulted in minimal conversation and eye contact. Peg, her co-worker, was much better at chatting up customers and building relationships.

"Yes, I work there," she said. "I'm sorry I don't remember…"

"That's all right," he said. "I'm sure you see a lot of customers. So tell me, do you like working there?"

Oh my God, he's starting a conversation. She repositioned her feet, which had been pointed toward the door, so she could better face him. "Yeah," she said. She realized it was a bland answer, so she quickly followed with, "I've always loved books. I just like to be around books."

"I do too," he said. "I've been a big reader ever since I was a kid. When I was growing up, my closet was filled with books because I couldn't fit them all in my room."

She said, "I have a giant bookcase in my apartment. It takes up the entire wall." She pointed to his notebook, which remained open on the table. "Do you like to write?"

"It's compulsive," he responded. "I can't help it."

"Are you published?"

"No," he said. "This is just for me. I don't share what I write."

Not intentionally, she thought to herself.

"What about you?" he asked. "Do you like to write?"

"Oh, I can't," she responded. "I don't have the gift. Either you have it or you don't. I just read. But I do envy writers. I think it must be such a great feeling to express yourself in words, on paper, exactly like you want."

"It never comes out exactly like you want," he said. "But when it's close, it's very gratifying." Then he added, "Maybe you'll find a way to express yourself through the guitar."

"Guitar?" She didn't follow.

"The guitar lessons."

"Yes, of course," she said quickly, internally kicking herself a good one. "I'm going to give it a shot anyway."

"It's good to try new things."

Their conversation fell into a natural flow. Ellen found him easy to talk with, already familiar with the rhythms of his voice.

His name was Charles Balun. He told her he worked as a senior systems manager at Technor. She recognized the name of his employer, one of Chicago's most prestigious new companies, located just a few blocks from the coffeehouse.

Before their conversation ended, he reached down and tore another blank page out of the notebook. Then he ripped the sheet neatly in half. He asked if they could exchange phone numbers. "I'd like to ask you out to dinner."

"Sure," she said in a tone ridiculously casual, given the multiple strokes and heart attacks she was experiencing.

She wrote down her phone number, watching the pen create the numbers as if by somebody else's hand. She gave the paper to him. "I'll be in tonight, if you want to give me a call."

"I will do," he said.

Ellen reported to work half an hour late.

Terri Smith, her boss, a patient woman with limits, reprimanded Ellen and called her behavior irresponsible.

Ordinarily, such a barbed statement would sting and hang heavy on Ellen's slender frame, but today she could feel no pain.

She couldn't even feel the floor beneath her feet.

Chapter Nine

Ellen moved through the bookstore with a new energy, chatting with customers with a bright smile on her face, abandoning her usual routine of hanging back in the rear aisles of low-traffic categories like reference. Her co-worker Peg took notice and asked, "So what's got you so hyper?"

Picturing Charles, Ellen blushed, as if Peg could view her thoughts. "I don't know. Just woke up on the right side of the bed, I guess."

"Whose bed?"

"Come on…"

"Nobody looks this happy unless they got laid or won the lottery. Or else you're quitting?"

"I'm not quitting. I like it here. I mean, I like the books."

"I'm right there with you," said Peg. "The books, not the customers." At the end of each shift, Peg would share her Rude Customer of the Day candidates, enacting the encounters with perfect mimicry.

As if on cue, an enormous woman in a puffy winter coat approached them, out of breath. "Excuse me, do one of you actually work here? I've just circled this entire store and I don't plan on doing it again. I can't find the diet books."

Ellen surprised Peg—and herself—by offering to help first. "Sure. Let me help you, ma'am. Follow me."

"You better share some of those lottery earnings," Peg called after her. "Remember your friends!"

After work, Ellen bought Mexican takeout and drove home, groaning at every small delay, including traffic lights that had the audacity to turn red. She didn't want to miss *the call*.

She felt like she was at least ten years younger. She tried to rationalize this rare buzz of excitement under her skin. "Am I this desperate for a date?" she asked aloud.

No, she answered herself. She had been asked out before. This one was just different. This young man reached deeper. He had stirred her up inside and won her over without even knowing of her existence. She had bonded with a stranger.

It was the red notebook.

Ellen surprised herself by hitting the horn to jolt the car in front of her into movement when it lingered at a green light for several seconds.

For the remaining blocks, she rehearsed a warm and carefree tone for the phone conversation. She knew she could sound tight and nervous. Her voice often wavered with uncertainty, fading up and down as if someone was playing with the volume.

"Hello, Charles," she said, realizing it was the first time she had spoken his name out loud. She repeated it several times to hear how it sounded on her lips. "Charles. Charles. Hi, Charlie!" She giggled to herself and found street parking not too far from her building. A good omen.

In her apartment, she ate at the kitchen counter, limiting herself to small bites. She didn't want to get caught with a mouth stuffed with food when the call came.

When the phone didn't ring during dinner, she quickly checked it for a dial tone—still working—and then tried to avoid a wave of pessimism. *Maybe he's not going to call. Maybe he had second thoughts.* She had his number, but the notion of phoning him for a date would require extra helpings of courage.

If only he wasn't so handsome… I'd take somebody half that good-looking just to get closer to the writer of that notebook.

The notebook remained in its drawer. She didn't want to take it out and start reading. She couldn't return to his voice and then get interrupted by a call from the real him. That was too much.

At eight fifteen p.m., she asked herself, *How late is too late for a call? Maybe he'll call tomorrow. Then I have to go through all of this anxiety for another twenty-four hours, except with the creeping feeling that maybe the call will never come.*

"Confidence," she said out loud, forceful, to push away all the other thoughts. "Confidence, Ellen…"

Not that she was looking at the clock or anything, but the phone rang at precisely eight twenty-two p.m.

She stared at the phone, letting him wait for a moment, before interrupting the third ring.

"Hello?" she said, feeling out of breath, as if she had dashed across the room rather than been standing directly over the phone. Nerves?

"Hello—is this—Ellen?"

"Yes, it is." It was *him.*

"Ellen, this is Charles. We met this morning at Pacific Coast Coffee…"

As if she had forgotten? She almost laughed. "Yes, of course. Hi, Charles."

"I hope I'm not, um, calling too late."

"No. Not at all. I'm up. I stay up late."

"Me too. I'm kind of a night owl. Um, anyway…"

There was a moment of silence, and it dawned on her that he sounded just as nervous as she felt.

"Would you…still like to…go out sometime?" His question probed cautiously.

"Sure," she said. In her mind, she added, *I'd love to,* but censored the words from reaching the phone for fear of sounding desperate. As long as he sounded nervous, she could play it cool.

They discussed several dinner possibilities, circling the globe of offerings on Chicago's North Side until landing on a Portuguese restaurant that neither had been to. "It'll be new for both of us," said Charles. "So if one of us doesn't like it, we can't blame the other."

"Deal," she said.

They set up a time to meet at her apartment on Friday night.

The entire call was finished in less than ten minutes. Not enough time to get to know one another better. But his interest in her had been verified. A dinner date had landed on her calendar.

She paced her living room for several minutes, tightly wound with nervous energy.

The notebook remained in her thoughts. The more its author became a real, flesh-and-blood person, the more she felt guilt-ridden about taking his personal property.

Charles had no idea that she already knew him more intimately than possibly anyone else. If he discovered that she had been reading his darkest feelings, no doubt he would be alarmed, possibly terrified.

She knew that's how she would feel if a stranger had been examining her own dark past without her knowledge, scrounging through the rubble of her personal pain and devastation.

For a moment, she resisted the urge to continue reading the journal. It was an invasion of privacy, wrong and disrespectful. It threw the relationship off balance. He would be exploring her for the first time through their dinner date, while she would have already learned so much about him.

She wanted to respect Charles and their relationship. But the magnetic pull of the journal proved too strong.

Within fifteen minutes of the end of their phone conversation, she had returned to its pages.

This time, as she read, she heard his voice. An even, deep tone, rich but unexcitable, broken by hesitations, an awareness of his own words, perhaps struggling for a comfort level or maybe just thoughtfully choosing a precise expression.

I begin today's journal entry with a heightened sense of despair that is not prompted by any recent occurrences. I belong in a better place as I continue to put more distance between my current state of affairs and the evil that destroyed my earlier years. But my wounds remain open, inviting new infections, incapable of healing.

I can heal you, Charles.

I can take care of my brother, Darren. I am there for him, twenty-four and seven, a loyalty that remains deep to the bone. But who will take care of me?

Darren cannot serve that role. He is too fragile, too volatile. I have no parents, no close friends. Held captive in my self-constructed cocoon, I long for a woman's touch and tenderness. I crave the nurturing I missed in my childhood. I need someone to hold me up, not like a crutch, but to empower me through love, respect and strength.

I am reaching out to you now, Charles. Can you feel my touch?

When I don't feel submersed in sadness, I am consumed by rage. I am certain that the origin of these mood swings is body chemistry, a stain on my brain, a fire that lives inside of me. I don't know what to do with the fury. I don't know what to do with the pain. I don't know what to do about the storms that wait for me in my nightly dreams. I only know I cannot stop them through drugs, alcohol or reason.

I'm here, Charles. Together we can conquer our demons. Our past doesn't have to dictate our future.

Sometimes I become so furious at everything around me, the impurity of my very existence, that there's no telling what I might do. Where is the relief? Who has the cure? When will I feel at peace?

We'll find happiness, Charles. We'll take each other there. We are exactly what each other needs.

Chapter Ten

Ellen realized that this was her third time looking at the card featuring the dancing monkeys with a "Go bananas on your birthday" punch line. She sighed and stuck it back in its slot in the rack.

The Book Shelf had a decent selection of greeting cards—one of the many ancillary items sold in the store to make up for sagging book sales.

However, nothing felt right today. The birthday cards were either too sappy, too silly or simply in bad taste. She considered settling for the most generic card possible and writing a long note — but what would she say?

To make matters worse, her mother's birthday was the following day. Even if she dropped a card in the mail this morning, it would arrive late.

Ellen gave the card rack a spin and watched the cartoons and colored words rotate like a roulette wheel. Should she reach out and pick one at random? *Eeny meeny miny mo...*

Ellen thought, *I should just call her.* It was a notion she often considered and rejected. After moving—escaping—to Chicago, she had not seen her mother at all, and had spoken to her on the phone only a few times. Ellen initiated the calls and often regretted them when the conversation turned shrill. She never invited her mother to visit her in Chicago. She didn't even offer an address.

The reason was simple. George might join her mother, and Ellen refused to ever see him again.

Ellen left the greeting card rack, wondering, *What am I going to do?*

She wished she could talk to Charles about this and seek his advice. Then she recalled a passage in the red notebook, sentiments about Charles's own mother, filled with yearning and regret. As it turned out, Charles had already spoken to Ellen on this subject.

———

When Ellen returned home that night, she threw down her purse and coat and immediately retrieved the journal. She brought it with her to the couch and found the passage she had remembered.

She read: *One of the saddest things about losing my mother when I was seven is the realization that I never expressed my love and appreciation toward her, stuck in that childhood mindset where everything is taken for granted and the world exists to serve you. My mother was a gentle, caring woman—far from perfect—but deep with good intentions. She's in a better place now. If she could only hear me, if she could read these words, I would tell her, loud and clear, the simple words that every living person needs to hear: I love you.*

Ellen had her answer. She called her mother, punching out the numbers quickly, before she could change her mind.

"Hello?" said the familiar voice, both far away and nestled in her ear.

"Mother, it's Ellen."

"Ellen?" She paused. "Ellen, are you okay?"

"I'm fine. I'm great, actually."

"Well…it's good to hear from you."

"I wanted to wish you a happy birthday."

"Is it…? I haven't…"

"It's tomorrow, Mom."

"Yes. Of course. I've been so busy…"

"It's good to be busy. What have you been busy with?"

"I've been going to church again, and I'm helping them with their rummage sale. And tonight, I'm having a little get-together for some of my friends, some of the ladies from work, we play cards. We take turns hosting."

"Mom, that's great." Ellen pictured her mother being social again—a big step forward. "What else is new?"

After a moment of silence, her mother said, "Ellen, he's gone."

"I beg your pardon?"

"George. He's gone. We're apart."

Ellen wanted to let out a cheer, but held it in and said, "What...where did he go?"

"We split up. It wasn't working. All those years, no ring. Throwing tantrums at every little thing. He's not very nice."

Jesus, Mom, it took you all this time to figure that out? thought Ellen.

"You made the right choice," said Ellen.

"I don't know." Her mother sighed.

"No. Trust me. You did." Ellen felt an urge to unleash the truth. She wanted to reveal George's true evil, the late-night abuse. The urge pressed inside her, but she held back. She had never discussed it with anyone. She couldn't open that door. There was too much anguish on the other side. She remained afraid.

"I think I'm better off now," said her mother.

"Definitely. He was a bad man, Mom."

"Perhaps." Ellen's mother changed the subject. "So what about you? How are you?"

"I'm doing really well."

"Work is good?"

"Work is very good. My health is good." Then Ellen couldn't resist adding, "Mom, I have a date tomorrow night. I think this guy might be someone really special."

"Really?" Her mother sounded surprised.

"I've gotten to know him...intimately...but not intimately like you're thinking...intimately as a person, his feelings, his philosophy..."

"Oh, Ellen..." said her mother, and the tone was not what Ellen was expecting. It sounded despondent.

"What? What's wrong?"

"Let me give you some advice, dear, from someone who has been there, a woman with a lot of experience..."

"Yes?"

"Stay away from men."

Ellen laughed.

"I'm not being funny," her mother said. "Jesus, Ellen, look what I've been through, first with your father, then with George. They have destroyed my health, they have ruined my sense of well-being and happiness. The only way to keep yourself true and together is to stay out of relationships. I'm not the only one who thinks this way. My new friend Bessie—"

"Mom, stop it," said Ellen.

"Buy yourself a vibrator."

"God, Mother!" Ellen wondered if her mother had been drinking. It was hard to tell; she tended to murmur, drunk or sober.

Ellen's mother continued, "You'll see. Whoever this young man is...he'll disappoint. He'll leave you. He'll hurt you. He's dangerous, they all are. He'll make you feel terrible in ways you never felt before."

Ellen couldn't stand hearing any more of it. "Mother, I need to go."

"Be strong, Ellen. Don't become dependent on him. Save yourself."

Ellen rushed the phone conversation to a conclusion. After she hung up, she paced the room.

How dare she try to tell me what to do? Just because she's never known true love doesn't mean I don't have a chance in this world.

Then Ellen realized she had failed to complete her one goal of the phone call. She had not said, "I love you."

Their relationship remained a mess.

Ellen turned her thoughts to Charles. She vowed that her mother's warnings wouldn't get in the way of her date. She would block them out entirely and with ease.

She was ready to hope again.

Chapter Eleven

Charles picked her up on time, seven o'clock on the nose, showing up in a long, dark coat, hands in pockets, smiling and fumbling for words. His shyness and unease comforted her—she no longer felt obligated to produce a slick front herself. They could be awkward together.

Upon his arrival, she felt an unusual urge to hug him. The journal had created a tremendous sense of familiarity. She reminded herself, *He knows nothing about me, while I've been learning everything about him.*

"Ready for Portugal?" he asked.

"I've got my passport," she joked.

"We'll grab a cab—is that okay?"

"Of course." She had her own car, but felt strange about offering to drive on a first date. Besides, parking in the neighborhood was a nightmare—a good way to start the date off on a note of aggravation.

The cab arrived and Charles opened the door. She had nearly circled the cab for the door on the other side before realizing *he's holding it open for me.*

She giggled, "Sorry," returning. Thanking him and climbing inside, she realized it had been a long time since she had dated—and a really long time since she had dated a *gentleman.*

The small backseat of the cab brought them closer together. She could feel her heart thumping. Her knees were brought up, long legs exposed. She wore a dark blue dress, so new that the price tags had been torn off less than an hour ago. He wore a charcoal gray sweater and black slacks. She wondered if the cabbie thought they looked cute together.

Charles gave the cabbie directions to the restaurant. The cab pulled away from the curb.

During the ten-minute ride, they skimmed a light conversation, commenting on the recent snow and promises of better weather later in the week.

At the restaurant, he again opened a door for her, but this time she was ready. Still, she nearly giggled nervously a second time. She caught a glimpse of herself in the glass and the reflection looked like someone else. When was the last time she had dressed up to look this good?

Her reddish-brown hair was fresh, unleashed and dropped forward. She had gray eyes, long limbs and a skinny teenager's build equipped with just enough feminine adult curves, nicely accented by the dress.

I can be pretty good looking, she thought, and it reminded her of the period in her life when she had enjoyed a good number of first dates.

Now just don't blow it with your personality.

Fortunately, with Charles, she didn't need to force a boisterous and flirtatious personality. He seemed to appreciate her more subdued approach. He wasn't exactly Mr. Extroverted himself.

They received menus and he studied the options before choosing the sautéed pork loin with clams. Ellen picked the broiled salmon with lemon dill sauce. She offered to share bites with him as long as he didn't have a cold.

"I don't have a cold," he said, almost defensively.

"I know, just joking."

He studied her. "You're supposed to smile when you make a joke."

"I wasn't smiling?" Ellen could hear Terri's voice at the Book Shelf: *Smile at the customers. You never smile. It's a bookstore, not a funeral home.*

"How's this?" She made a big grin, silly and exaggerated.

"Now that's a smile."

"Okay, your turn."

"For what?"

"A smile. You're pretty serious, too."

He thought about it for a moment. Then he held a hand in front of his mouth. He lifted the hand to show a sudden, crazy smile, then dropped the hand as if to immediately conceal it.

She laughed and said, "You're weird," quickly adding, "I'm still *joking*."

The goofy conversation seemed to relax them both. Subsequent drinks also helped. As he became more fleshed out in three dimensions, a real human being behind the words in the journal, her physical attraction to him grew. She watched him from across the table, taking in his dark, soulful eyes and broad, square shoulders. During her first drink, she imagined kissing his lips. She imagined him kissing her throat. She surprised herself with the passionate imagery in her mind, embarrassed that it was taking place as they engaged in a casual conversation.

They talked for a while about their jobs. He was a high-level manager at a hot new technology company, which impressed her. She talked about the bookstore. Then, during the main course, she tried to steer him toward the deeper territory covered in his journal.

"Where did you grow up? Have you always lived in Chicago?"

"No. I've been all over. It might be easier to list the places where I haven't lived."

"Your parents moved a lot?"

"Pretty much."

"What kind of work did your dad do?"

"Different things."

"Like what?"

"Insurance."

She could tell they were entering an area of difficulty from his short answers and elusive eye contact. She tried to probe deeper into his past, but his answers grew more vague until he changed the subject altogether. He randomly made a comment about a woman's hat at a nearby table, then said something about the music playing.

That's all right, thought Ellen. *We'll get you to open up over time. There's no rush. We'll get to our respective histories. We'll find that lonely place in each other's hearts that draws us close.*

After dinner, he suggested drinks at a bar around the corner, Poppy's. She quickly agreed—it was too early to call it a night and she didn't feel comfortable going to his place on a first date—or to her place, either, for that matter, although she had cleaned it just in case.

At Poppy's, the noise from the crowd and a blaring Bulls game caused them to search out a booth in the back. They ordered beers and Ellen realized that she was going to consume more alcohol tonight than she had in a long time. Her thin frame offered low tolerance, so she tried to pace herself without getting too far behind Charles's drink input.

He asked her more questions about the bookstore, and that neatly segued into a conversation about favorite books. He confessed to collecting a lot of thrillers, murder mysteries and true crime. She told him about her favorites: historical romance, fantasy and some "chick lit".

"When I met you at the coffeehouse, you were writing," she said. "Do you like to write?"

"I do," he replied, then turned it back on her. "What about you? Working in a bookstore, surrounded by all those books. Are you an aspiring author?"

"I'm not much of a writer. I wish I was better at it. I used to write a lot of stories when I was younger, but I stopped. I'd like to do more writing. Even if it was just poems or short stories."

"So write," he encouraged. "If you have a pen and paper, you're all set. It's the easiest pursuit in the world. You don't even have to share it with anyone."

She seized the opening. "What do *you* write about?"

"All sorts of things."

"Like what?"

"I don't know. Whatever I feel like. It doesn't matter."

He was being cagey. She wanted to know more about the voice in the journal. Feeling relaxed and uninhibited from the drinks, she attempted to bring the conversation back to his personal history. "So tell me more about your past. Why don't you like to talk about it?"

He appeared startled. His jaw hung and he seemed to search for words. He finally shrugged and said, "I have some baggage," with a weak smile.

"Don't we all?" she asked, hoping her tone offered reassurance.

"I know, but...let's not go there. I'm having a good time."

"I am, too, Charles."

He appeared surprised. "Really? I know I've been babbling a lot tonight. I'm kind of boring. I haven't...been out much. I'm a little rusty at this dating thing."

"Hey, so am I," she said.

He looked at her for a long, silent moment and then said, "You're very beautiful." It sent a shiver through her. Her first impulse, strangely, was to cry. But she swallowed it back even as tears threatened to well in her eyes. *Don't mess up your mascara!*

"Thank you," she said, and the words came out flat, not at all as she intended.

A young waitress in a blue Poppy's shirt appeared and asked if they wanted another drink.

"I'm good," said Ellen quickly, head still spinning from Charles's comment. The evening's intensity had caught up with her — or perhaps the extra drinks. She felt both wired and exhausted. In a short period of time, she had met the man behind the journal, her first date in a long time, fallen deeper for his good looks and kind eyes, probed into his secret past, and been told she was...*beautiful?*

She needed to go home. She felt anxiety rising inside. If she stayed with him much longer, she risked getting nauseous or stupid or both. So much had been achieved in one night. She wanted to remove herself, reflect, regroup. *Do it now, before you blow it.*

"Charles, I've really enjoyed tonight," she said. "But it's getting late and I'd like to go home."

She could sense a slight sag in his reaction. "Oh. Sure."

"I'm just tired, that's all," she quickly offered. "I'd—I'd like to do this again sometime."

He straightened up. "Yes. Me, too. Good."

They returned to her apartment in a cab, barely speaking in the backseat. She felt blasted by one of her old waves of insecurity. Where did it come from? Why now? She was afraid to speak because she didn't feel confident that the right words and sentiments would come out.

When they pulled up in front of her building, Charles said, "Let me walk you to your door."

"You want me to wait?" grumbled the driver.

Charles looked at Ellen.

"No," said Charles.

At that moment, Ellen knew that Charles was going to kiss her.

My mouth is dry, she panicked. *I'm trembling. I am so lame.*

Charles paid the driver and they got out of the vehicle. The cab left right away, red rear lights vanishing around a corner.

Charles walked with Ellen to her building entrance. They stopped at the glass door to the vestibule and faced each other.

"I would have asked him to wait," he said. "But I don't like an audience."

She smiled—big, genuine and spontaneous—no effort behind it.

Charles leaned in and kissed her. She responded quickly. *Be receptive. Prove to him that this is not the end.*

A rush of warmth traveled her body, tingling up into her scalp. She felt his gentle lips. His hand touched the back of her shoulder. She brought her hands toward him and touched his waist.

He broke it off after a minute, but remained close. "Have a good night," he said.

"I already did."

He smiled and turned. He started down the walk.

She entered her building, then watched him from inside the vestibule. He waved at her before advancing out of view.

Her hands trembled with so much excitement that it took her a minute to get a firm grip on her keys and unlock the door.

Once inside her garden apartment, she paced. She replayed the highlights of the evening in her head, bits of dialogue, moments of contact. She felt a rush of energy.

For the first time in a long while she felt all of her senses brought to life.

While Charles had departed in the flesh, he very much remained a presence in her apartment. She ran to the desk drawer and pulled out the red journal.

She kissed the cover, then laughed at herself for doing it.

She jumped on the couch and opened the journal to her bookmark.

Tonight she had experienced the handsome, quiet, outward Charles.

Now she was returning to the deep, intense, inner Charles. A man with secrets, scars and darkness. A wise heart that knew true hurt. He may have kept his emotions in check during the date, but now they revealed themselves in plain, black-and-white penmanship.

Charles wrote: *Sometimes I feel on the verge of tears, a sadness triggered by the most innocent moment, something mundane that drags out everything I have tried to suppress. A school bus of small faces. The smell of a long-ago cologne. A father and son playing catch in a driveway. An old song bringing memories of an AM radio smuggled under the bed covers to block out shouts from down the hall.*

Yesterday, I had another run-in with Darren. I fear I am losing some of my influence over his behavior. Above all, he needs to protect himself from himself. Where I feel sorrow, he feels rage. Where I can channel the pain inward, he lashes out in all directions. He is losing the basic grounding to function in society. While I have held on to rational thought, his fingers are losing their grasp. We are so very different yet inevitably the same. We are two sides of a coin, fused by a common experience.

Perhaps now is the time to revisit the day that changed our lives forever. The climax and starting point to this narrative. The destruction that gave birth to a thousand nightmares.

When I embarked on this journal, it was an experiment with an ambitious goal of self-discovery but no sure formula to get there. In the course of these two hundred pages, I have been able to extract and unwind elements of my construction in hopes of identifying the stranger that lives inside of me. I have established a process and voice with the simplest of tools. I have reached a degree of some clarity, but solutions remain elusive. I have not improved my mental state of affairs. Deterioration and fragmentation persist. In truth, my explorations to date have been a warm-up. Now is the time to leap into the mouth of the monster.

I have introduced the players. I have established a storyline. I have described the conflicts and escalated the tension. Perhaps now we can ride out the pivotal scene?

I am seven years old. I am playing with Darren in our bedroom. The shouts and screams from our parents have never been this loud, raw and passionate. Their bodies thump against walls. Our home is breaking apart in explosions of violence: fists, kicking, broken glass and toppled furniture, a war zone.

We can hear everything in our room. I desire to hide in the attic, wrap my head in pillows, climb out the window, or hang myself in the basement. Darren presses his hands against his ears until tears squeeze from his eyes.

The noise crescendos, leading to the most piercing wail either one of us has ever heard. I know at that moment that the terror in our home has reached another pinnacle. When the sounds of my parents' enraged battle shrivels to a single, muffled sob, I know that there is an end, a finality, and I can only hope that it is a joint realization that all of this horror needs to go away, consume itself, evaporate.

Darren and I leave the bedroom and head down the stairs, drawn to the sound of the strange crying coming from our father. When we find him, he is doubled up in a ball, like an infant, eyes wild, face scratched, white T-shirt torn. We see a butcher knife tossed across the floor, inches from where our mother rests limply, one shoe off, not moving. We see huge cuts like bloody lips grimacing through her dress. She soaks in a pool of red.

My father faces us, his features pink and puffy, a madman spitting out two words with a guttural ejection: "Get…OUT."

For the next few days, I will try to wash that image out of my eyes with soap and water until I can no longer stand the burning.

I will never speak to my father again. I will feel nothing when many years later I discover he has been killed in prison, larynx crushed by a broom handle in a violent fight with another inmate.

I will fail to shed even a single tear.

Chapter Twelve

Ellen could not shake the image of seven-year-old Charles and his brother entering the kitchen and discovering the violent stabbing death of their mother at the hands of their father. Even after Ellen had returned the notebook to the drawer and finished her glass of red wine, which usually made her tired, she could not settle her trembling. The journal's words remained in her head and she still pictured the scene as he had described it, down to the splashes of blood on the cabinet doors.

Charles had experienced unbearable horror. It put her own childhood trauma to shame. How could she continue to feel sorry for herself in light of this man's grief?

Ellen knew that most women would drop the relationship after making such a discovery. It would be easier to leave than to stay. Your average twenty-something gal—cute, bubbly, looking for a good time—would jump to other options. How many young singles would pursue a romance with someone burdened by such terrible emotional baggage? Even though Charles could not be blamed for the evil in his family, he would be considered tainted. Damaged goods. His dark childhood, suicidal desires, and continued sorrow and angst would be a distraction that would overpower the passion.

For Ellen, the inverse was true. She felt closer to Charles than ever before. She could fully understand why he would not want to share his past with her at this early stage in the relationship. She sympathized with his reluctance to talk about the pain.

Retiring to bed, slipping beneath the cool sheets, she imagined reaching for him and finding his warm body. She held him tight, two weakened souls drawing newfound strength from each other's intimate understanding. They could connect on a level few others could.

Swimming in and out of her dreams that night, Charles confronted her without words. In a jumble of time and place, he appeared in the apartment where she had once lived with her mother. Standing before her, he grasped the bottom of his sweater and brought it up, peeling it off over his head. He revealed his strong upper body, sculpted and sensual. He pointed to ugly slashes across the flesh, over his heart. She did not flinch. She touched the scars with her fingertips, kissed him, and began the healing.

———

Ellen arrived earlier than usual to Pacific Coast Coffee. She had dressed up, spent extra time on her hair and makeup, and abandoned her usual frumpy workday wardrobe. She sat near the front, facing the door, legs crossed, skirt pulled back to the knees, eyelashes thickened, hair brushed full.

She knew that she might run into him.

She sipped her latte, pretended to read the latest edition of *New City*, and glanced up every time the door opened with a whoosh of cold winter air. She stayed later than usual, accepting Terri's irritated glance when she entered the Book Shelf at five after nine.

Terri appeared ready to reprimand Ellen, but then switched gears, taking in her change of appearance. "Look at you. You must be going someplace special after work."

"No," said Ellen. "Just home."

"Do you have a hot date?" asked Peg, appearing beside Terri, a wide grin pushing back her freckled cheeks.

Ellen felt herself blush. "No."

"She's been really chipper lately," said Peg. "Something's up. I'll get it out of her."

"Well, transfer all that good enthusiasm to the customers," said Terri. "I don't want to see anybody enter this store without a greeting and offer to help."

Ellen nodded, ready to search out patrons.

"And one more thing," said Terri, pointing to Ellen's wrist. "You have a watch. Use it. Don't turn me into a pest."

"Sorry," said Ellen.

"If you have a special reason for coming in late, we can talk."

"No special reason," said Ellen. "I just got off to a late start."

"It's her first day wearing eye shadow, give her a break," said Peg.

"Very funny," responded Ellen. From anyone else, the comment would sting. But Peg was just being Peg.

"Enough," said Terri. "Let's split up."

Ellen and Peg drifted apart to opposite sides of the store and then rejoined in the back, out of Terri's view.

"Okay, she's busy," said Peg. "Now talk."

"About what?"

"You know."

"I don't know."

Peg moved closer. "I'm not gay, so don't take this the wrong way, but you're looking hot. It's like another person walked in this morning. Look at you, you've been hiding a really nice bod. I'd have to stop eating and work out twice a day to get like that. Nice genes, girl. Both my parents have pot bellies, so you know where I'm headed. You really should spruce up like this more often."

"I don't like to draw attention to myself."

"So what's different about today?"

Ellen could feel herself blushing again, a warmth across her cheeks. She sensed Peg studying her and turned away.

"Aw, c'mon," said Peg. "I tell you all about my stupid life. You get all sorts of juicy details. Like that time I laughed so hard I peed all over myself at my sister's wedding. And all my bad date stories, like that guy who burped tacos in my mouth when we were kissing. You owe me, sister."

"Okay," said Ellen. She took in a deep breath. "It's a guy. But it's early. I don't want to...you know."

"Jinx it by talking about it?"

"Exactly."

"Maybe that's my problem," said Peg. "So does this guy have a name?"

"Charles."

"Charles." Peg frowned. "That's kind of formal. Why not Charlie or Chuck? Is he from the North Shore? Sounds like he has money. Does he have nice shoes?"

Ellen laughed. "All right. That's all you're getting today."

"A name? That's hardly anything. Where's the good stuff? Is he a good kisser? What color are his eyes? Is his belly button an innie or an outie?"

Ellen latched on to a customer to assist. For the rest of the day, Peg followed Ellen around the store, trying to extract more information about Charles. Ellen remained tight-lipped, as if releasing information would diminish her excitement.

"Keeping me in suspense will not make me go away!" said Peg.

As soon as Ellen returned to her apartment, she felt the red notebook's presence. It seemed to follow her around the living room, as if it could watch her through the drawer, using Charles's eyes. She felt increased guilt over possessing it. She was close to the end. She knew that she could finish it tonight if she stayed up late.

Ellen ate a simple pasta-and-salad dinner at the small table in her kitchen and planned the notebook's return to Charles. She plotted to bring the journal to the coffeehouse early the next morning in order to "find" it for him.

She drafted a short script to read when she called him.

"Charles, it's Ellen. I'm at Pacific Coast Coffee. I think I found something that belongs to you. It's a notebook. It was buried under a stack of magazines. It looks like your handwriting. I didn't read any of it."

She crossed out the final line. It was too dishonest. If pressed, maybe she would admit to glancing at some of it—reading a few pages before she realized it was private and closed the covers. But even that was totally dishonest.

I'm going to have to lie to him. Great way to start off the relationship, Ellen!

Ellen cleaned the dinner dishes, then prepared her couch with pillows and a blanket. Her heartbeat jumped with anticipation. She walked over to the desk drawer and pulled it open. The red notebook cover stared up at her like an old friend.

She reached down and took a hold of it.

One more dance, Charles?

She shut the drawer and brought the notebook to the couch. She had marked her place with her tattered bookmark from childhood.

Ellen began reading, her eyes moving down the page at a deliberate pace, anxious to take in the writing, but not wanting to rush, savoring every word and absorbing each emotion.

A revelatory clarity has yet to escape the fog. At times, I am consumed by overwhelming anxiety that leads me to blackouts, sucked into segments of space and time where I have no recall. I am lost in my own life, drawn back to childhood confusion, searching constantly for that parent or guardian or lover or friend who will lead the way. Short dips into therapy and counseling have not been effective means to self-discovery and happiness. I need someone to take my hand without motivations of billable hours, professional gain or smug self-satisfaction.

My stomach fell ill again today. Sometimes it is a miracle I can keep food down. I am fascinated that the people around me see an ordinary and bland member of the human race when I know that I am anything but. I remain broken, disassembled parts, a curiosity unto myself. I used to fool myself that love could solve…

The phone rang.

Ellen tossed the notebook off her lap like a child caught with a hand in the cookie jar.

For a moment, the prospect of two Charleses — one on the page, one on her phone — threw her. She froze and forced the transition in her mind.

Ellen caught the phone on the fourth ring, her last chance before the answering machine kicked in.

"Hello…?

"Ellen?" spoke the familiar voice.

"Hi, Charles."

He sounded hesitant, as if still struggling for a reason to call. She was growing used to his conversation starters—fumbling and uncertain until he found solid footing. "I just thought I'd call to say hi. I hope you don't mind."

"Not at all. I'm happy you called. How are you?"

"Good," he said quickly in a flat tone, as if forcing the word out.

She told him, "I really had a nice time Friday night."

"I did, too. That was a good restaurant. I want to go back there sometime and try some of the other dishes."

"I know. Me too." As she spoke, a horrible image flickered in the corner of her eye: Charles's gruesome childhood discovery, replayed across her living room. She saw the fallen body of his murdered mother, his father weeping, the bloody butcher knife…

Ellen shut her eyes to drive the images away.

"Listen, I'm sorry if I acted a little weird the other night," Charles said. "I'm sort of rusty. I haven't dated a lot in the past few years. I'm pretty quiet. I work with people who are older. I don't go out all the time. I'm a bit of a homebody."

"I can relate," she said, thinking, *I can relate in so many ways you aren't even aware of.*

Ellen was determined to get him to open up. She wanted to hear him address the personal history he described so vividly and passionately in his journal. She knew that if she could prompt such a breakthrough, their relationship would become deeper and closer.

"I haven't dated a lot, either, if you want to know the truth," said Ellen.

"Really? A pretty girl—I'm sorry, *woman*—like you?"

Her heart danced inside. "Thank you, but I don't know about that. When I was in high school, they called me Olive Oyl because of my skinny arms and legs and long neck."

"Whoever said that was a jerk."

"I didn't take it seriously," she said, which was definitely not true.

"I got teased a lot when I was in high school," he said.

"What about?" she asked him.

"Oh, just, you know, the usual stupid stuff."

"Like what? What do boys tease each other about in high school?"

"I don't remember. It's not worth remembering." He was retreating.

She said, "I wasn't very happy back in high school. It was a pretty melodramatic time in my life."

"Everything is crazy and amplified."

"I was really…depressed a lot back then," she said. "I mean *really* depressed."

As Ellen talked into the cordless phone, she paced the room. She began turning off the lights one by one. *Click…Click…*

The dark made it easier to talk about pain. Draining visibility from the apartment somehow brought Charles closer.

Click.

As she turned off the final light, plunging the room into complete blackness, she said, "I used to think about killing myself."

There was silence on the other end.

Now is your chance, Charles. This is your opening. Please…

"That's really terrible," he said.

"Did you ever feel so down that you wanted to just, you know, put it all down in a suicide note and leave the planet?" Her tone was light, almost encouraging him to agree.

He held steady. "Not really. I mean…I would feel down, but not to the point where I would do something like that."

"Or even just think about it?"

"No."

She felt disappointed. He was so candid in his notebook. Why wouldn't he open up now, over the phone? Couldn't he see the intimacy in this evening conversation, holed up in their respective dwellings, two voices engaged in a private dance, not having to look one another in the eye? She wanted so badly to share secrets with him…

She said, "If I tell you something, do you promise that it won't scare you away?"

"Boy," he laughed. "That's a loaded question."

"No, it's just something about my past. A long time ago. But it's part of what made me such a messed-up teen. It's my parents. My parents really screwed me up."

"I can relate to that," said Charles. "Without a doubt."

Ellen thought, *he's emerging.*

"Tell me more," said Charles. "What was it about your parents that messed you up?"

"Well, some if it was pretty typical. They fought all the time, they got divorced. I never saw them happy together. Just battling. Screaming. Violent even."

She paused, offering him another opening.

He didn't say anything.

So she continued. "After they divorced, my mom had something like a nervous breakdown, and she was always on pills, which actually made her worse instead of better, and she got involved with this guy…" Ellen realized that her own story was getting harder to push out. She sat down on the living room floor, surrounded by darkness.

She could hear Charles's breathing on the other end.

She said, "Her boyfriend was pretty sick, it turned out. He abused me…"

"Hit you?"

"Worse than that."

"Oh," Charles said. He understood. He gently asked, "How old were you?"

"Young." She felt tears on her cheeks. The pain of the memory was catching up with her. She had never talked about it out loud like this before. Not to her mother, not to anyone. "It was…traumatic beyond belief."

Damn it, Charles, I gave you this opportunity. Open up for me. I know what happened to you and your brother. I know about your parents.

"I'm so sorry," was all he said.

"I shouldn't go into this," she said, swallowing back any further tears. "I mean, you couldn't possibly relate…"

"Not exactly, but maybe a little."

"What do you mean?" She felt her heart pounding. Was he ready to reveal his past?

"Well, I once knew a girl who had an older sister who was abused by her uncle."

Seconds after feeling her hopes rise, Ellen felt swamped by disappointment. She decided to give up, at least for now. What did she expect? They had gone out on only one date. Maybe as the relationship continued…

"Hey," she said, injecting a cheery tone, abruptly switching gears. "How did we get down this path? Talk about a bummer. Let's talk about something a little more upbeat."

"That would be a good idea," he agreed.

"Here's a funny story. We caught a guy shoplifting at the bookstore today. He had like four books shoved down the front of his pants. He could barely walk. We caught him at the door. Then he tells us he was planning on paying for them, he just forgot. And they were all science fiction paperbacks with dragons on the front."

They shared some more stories about their day and the conversation ended on a high note: Charles asked Ellen out to dinner and drinks on Saturday night.

After the call, Ellen checked the clock. Their conversation had lasted nearly ninety minutes. After a bumpy start, they had found a smooth, comfortable rapport, despite only skimming the surface of each other's lives. There would be more opportunities to lift the layers.

Now she was pressed to stay up even later to accomplish her goal of finishing the notebook. There weren't too many pages left. She knew she could do it.

Ellen returned to the couch, where the notebook remained hidden under the blanket, as if Charles could have seen into the room from the phone.

She took it and curled up against a pile of pillows. She quickly returned to the point where she had left off.

The words on the page came to life with Charles's voice still fresh in her ears. He spoke again about his brother, Darren.

I went looking for Darren today. I continue to worry for his mental health. His absence frightens me because I can envision all too well his behavior and the potential for dangerous predicaments.

I love and fear my brother. We recognize ourselves in each other's eyes. We share an experience we can never shed. We must suffer together. We must watch out for one another and protect each other by any means necessary.

If I must have Darren committed to a psychiatric hospital, I am prepared to take that action, even if it rips out my heart.

———

As Ellen read well past midnight, the journal's handwriting became more rushed and careless. Charles became obsessed with finding his missing brother, frightened by his disappearance and fearing the worst. His words flowed fast and furious. Then she read:

I came home today to find Darren in my living room. I do not know how he got in. He boasted of violence. He claimed he had attacked innocent people in the park, hurting them, seeking satisfaction in creating pain and fear. He told me that he could only cope with his rage by turning it on others. He ridiculed me for being "passive" and "resigned" to feeling sorry for myself. He said I would self-destruct while he grew stronger.

He insulted and baited me until I could take no more. I told him I was going to confine him to an institution where he could do no harm. I told him that if what he told me was true, I would call the police. The violence had to stop.

In a flash, like the crack of a thunderbolt, we fought. We attacked each other as if tearing into a hated part of ourselves. I finally pulled a knife on him. He fled my home. Now I fear he is out there, somewhere, dangerous, performing acts of random violence to satisfy his sick soul.

Ellen's heart pounded as she read a long, rambling passage lamenting Darren's mental deterioration. It went on for several pages, panicked.

Then she encountered a blank page. She stared at the whiteness.

Had the journal ended?

She turned the blank page and the writing started up again.

She read:

Hello there.

It's Darren.

I have enjoyed reading the drivel that drips from the pen of my brother. He feels that he is stronger than I. He believes he can control me, that he is somehow superior.

He is wrong on all counts. He is sad, pathetic and misguided.

To prove my point most emphatically, I have beaten him into submission. I have sent him away for a while, crippled his abilities, and there is only me. I will take over these pages, your "guest host." I will smear my bile across this journal. I will share with you, dear reader, a lifetime of unrelieved agony and all of its consequences. I will bare the truth that my brother can only allude to.

It's so easy.

I operate without conscience.

I move anonymous among the masses.

Tonight was a milestone in the madness. It was decades in the making. In the dark of the night, I slaughtered a complete stranger. A human being became an object for my manipulation. I made an innocent young woman die. I lashed out like an animal upon weaker prey. I fed on the flavor of blood like a starving man feasts on food. I left no witnesses. I felt no regret.

There is no going back. I will deliver more hurt to the world. It tastes good. The world has fucked me for too many years and now I fuck the world. I have found the simplest answer to my unrelieved agony. How could I not see it before? Always in front of me, always so plain. I merely altered my role, and therefore my destiny. I am no longer a victim. I am in total control. I am more powerful than life itself because I can personify death. I am rising above it all. The ugly in my mind has manifested itself into action. On this day, a killer is born.

Let the victims begin.

With those four words, the journal ended.

Ellen stared at the last sentence in horror, the notebook stuck in her sweaty grasp.

The intrusion of Darren's narrative came from nowhere, a shock striking her deep in the heart.

But the most horrifying aspect of this new voice and its murderous confessions went beyond the prose. It lived in the penmanship staring back at her. Darren may have taken over the journal from Charles.

But the handwriting remained the same.

Chapter Thirteen

Linda Geesin thought about the red clogs for most of the afternoon and into the early evening. It gave her something to focus on outside of the checkout counter routine at Sunrise Groceries. The Swedish-style platform shoes had wood bottoms, red leather, and cost sixty dollars minus twenty percent off through Friday. If ten percent of sixty was six, then twenty was twelve, and sixty minus twelve was…forty-eight. Plus tax. Sixty was pricey, but forty-eight…that entered the realm of possibility.

She had seen the clogs in the window of Sole Mates, a small shoe store between her job and apartment, the previous morning. She had gone inside the store and confirmed that they had size eight in red. But she hadn't bought them right away. She was more disciplined than that. She was not an impulse shopper—not like the customers she saw in the grocery store who grabbed random candy and magazines off the racks in the check-out line, items they had never intended to buy when they came in.

Linda typically gave herself a twenty-four-hour cooling period, minimum, to analyze whether or not she really wanted particular merchandise. For the clogs, the cooling period had ended earlier that day, and she still wanted them.

The clogs created a nice picture in her head, a daydream to fill the short moments between customers. The shoes helped distract her from the stress and tension in her hands, arms, shoulders and neck that came from moving an endless parade of groceries across the scanner. Another clerk had once shared stretching exercises with her and recommended a better standing posture to relieve some of the aches, but it didn't bring Linda more comfort than the aspirin she kept in her pants pocket, under the purple apron. Sometimes, on a particularly bad day, she took two or three. A bad day usually meant customer problems: out-of-control toddlers provoking hot-tempered parents, glitches with processing credit or debit cards, arguments over change or expired coupons, slow check-writers, and demands to discount less-than-perfect produce, as if she was in a position to barter.

Through it all, she smiled sweetly until her face hurt. Usually smiles could offset the anger. She rarely argued with the customers. She simply brought in a manager to take over. Most of the time that meant Marty, who was cranky and less patient. The good cop/bad cop routine would go into effect.

Linda rarely complained, even when Marty repeatedly placed her at the checkout counter nearest to the sliding doors, which meant frequent blasts of cold winter air and listening to the shrieks, squeals and crashes of shopping carts rolling in and out of the store.

Every day started fresh and ended in exhaustion, even though she mostly stood in place.

Commonly, her "breaks" meant trading off with an employee working the floor. She didn't mind taking inventory, stocking shelves, cleaning spills or removing torn bags of chips and cookies where patrons had helped themselves to a snack. At least it offered some variety.

Today the clogs saved her day from disappearing completely into the mundane. She was actually glad she hadn't bought them yet. Then what would fill her mind? What would fill her mind *after* she bought the shoes? She wondered if Marty would let her bring Sudoku puzzles to the cash register to work on during idle periods, as long as it didn't distract anyone or take attention away from customers.

She thought about Sudoku puzzles a while longer, then imagined the red clogs on her feet, fitting snug, feeling fine.

At ten p.m., Marty crashed the sliding doors shut and locked them. Linda felt a small lift. She knew that when she reported to work the next day at two p.m., she would be wearing her prized new purchase. The thought gave her a brief flutter of pleasure.

She went into the back room, which always smelled like rotten food, and traded her purple apron for her orange parka. She engaged in a flat exchange of goodbyes with her co-workers. Marty stood waiting for them at the front entrance with his big ring of keys. He allowed them to slip through a narrow opening one by one, quickly shutting and locking the doors again after each departure, as if a mob waited outside to rush the entrance.

"Goodbye," muttered Marty as Linda left the store. *Whoosh-crash!* went the sliding doors behind her. She stepped onto the sidewalk. The cold air chilled her legs and face. She pulled the hood over her head to warm her ears. Her brother had once told her that she looked like a child when she wore the hood. She had a small frame and a soft face. The loose-fitting parka obscured her adulthood. She didn't care if she looked like a little kid. The parka was warm. Chicago was freezing.

She moved swiftly during the walk to her apartment building. The frenzied activity of the city blurred into three-second glimpses: other pedestrians, *walk/don't walk* lights, traffic sliding past, and dimmed storefront displays.

I wonder if the clogs will be noisy on the hardwood floors of my apartment.

I need to buy another Sudoku book.

I'm hungry. When I get home, I'm making soup. Chicken and rice.

I wish my brother lived closer.

I think my right eye is stronger than my left. I need a new prescription for my glasses.

What if they sold the last pair of red clogs in my size?

She walked past Sole Mates, closed and dark. The red clogs remained in the window. She would have stopped for a closer look, but there was a large homeless man near the entrance, leaning against the bricks, barking the same six words over and over, like a tape loop. "Spare change? Good day to you. Spare change? Good day to you."

Linda frequently saw him around the neighborhood. He was heavyset with deadened eyes and missing front teeth that highlighted his incisors like fangs. He scared her, especially when he lingered near her apartment building. He was certainly crazy and probably dangerous. Occasionally she saw him shouting at traffic, waving a fat fist like a club.

She kept moving, past him and the shoe store, and formulated her game plan for the next day.

I need to get to Sole Mates right when it opens. What if I've waited too long? I'm not the only person with size-eight feet. Don't you remember what happened with the vest that was on sale at Benson's? After the twenty-four-hour cooling period, it was gone. Sometimes there's something to be said for impulse shopping.

Linda reached her apartment building. She looked to see if the homeless man was following her. It was one of her fears. He could be a rapist or robber.

But she didn't see him. Just a few normal-looking people walking on the sidewalk.

She entered the building's vestibule and tossed back her hood. She flattened her hair with a swipe of her hand. For a moment, her glasses fogged. She took them off, but her naked vision wasn't much better. When her glasses cleared, she put them back on. She checked the bin under the lineup of mailboxes to see if she had any magazines or catalogues.

None. Somebody named Beth Lawter had received a bicycling magazine. The Polish woman with the long last name had received a scrapbooking catalogue. Without even looking at the labels on the remaining periodicals, she knew they weren't for her. Sports. Business. Cooking.

At the bottom of the bin, everyone had received a green flyer promoting kitchen and bathroom remodeling services. No doubt those would remain in the bin until someone took the initiative to toss them.

She took out her key chain and used a small, almost toy-like key to open her mailbox. One item, the phone bill, greeted her. She took it and shut the mailbox.

As Linda unlocked and opened the heavy interior door leading to the staircase, someone entered the building behind her. Startled by the noise, she stole a quick glance—and was instantly relieved. It was a young man, handsome and professional looking. He smiled politely at her. She had not seen him before. Then again, she didn't know many of her neighbors.

"Hi," he said.

"Hi," she responded. He was coming her way, so she held the door open for him.

"Thanks," he said.

She headed up the carpeted stairs, her tired thoughts falling back on her top three preoccupations of the moment: soup, Sudoku, clogs.

If the red clogs in her size were sold, would she settle for another color? Navy blue?

Linda reached the third floor and proceded to her apartment. She unlocked her door with a twist of her wrist, resulting in the familiar, hard click of the bolt. She continued to think about the clogs. At that moment in time, nothing else mattered but getting those shoes. She turned the handle and pushed the door open—

Abruptly the door smacked her in the face with a loud thud at the same time that she felt a forceful shove from behind. A blast of air expelled from her lungs. A second blow sent her tumbling into her apartment, the floor rushing up to meet her. She landed on the heels of her hands, skidding on the floorboards.

"Hey!" she shouted, an involuntary exclamation, somewhere between surprise and fear. Dazed, she flipped over on her back to see the source of the blows.

A faceless figure stood in the doorway. He kicked her hard in the legs, sending her farther into the room. He wore a dark green ski mask, erasing his features, except for two eyes, a nose and teeth.

"Move," he said, and he kicked her again, this time aiming higher, into her ribs. She shrieked and scrambled away from further blows, which gave him the space he needed to shut the door behind him.

He secured the deadbolt with a loud snap.

He stepped toward her.

She started to scream, but the scream cut off as he fell on top of her, his knee digging deep into her stomach.

She thrashed under him, her head bouncing against the floor in the struggle. Her glasses fell askew. Short glimpses of her apartment flashed before her eyes—familiar things, symbols of home and security crashing into a brand-new context as terror spun a web around her.

When she realized she could not escape the crushing weight on top of her, she used her draining energy to exhale words.

"I'll give you my money please don't hurt me—"

He yanked the zipper apart on her orange parka, splitting the coat open to place a hand on her breast.

"Don't, don't rape—" she said.

The brown eyes stared back at her from inside the green wool mask. The nostrils flared, hissing. The lips curled upward in a smile.

Linda saw a blur of movement and then experienced the worst pain of her life.

Clutching at the fire in her abdomen, she tried to scream but could only choke.

The man in the ski mask stood, removing his weight. The deep stinging continued to electrify her entire body.

He walked across her apartment, evenly spaced footsteps on the hardwood floor, until he stopped at her living room window. He shut the blinds, tugging on the cord with his left hand.

She saw the bloody knife in his right hand.

She began to crawl across the floor and realized she was sliding in liquid—her own blood. She reached the coffee table and used the edge to pull herself up. She could see the blood pouring from her body. Her breathing turned shallow and rapid. Her face felt cold and sweaty.

When the attacker in the ski mask returned, Linda fought back with the only weapon within her grasp—the television remote. She struck it against the side of his head and it exploded into plastic pieces, the batteries bouncing across the room.

He flinched for a moment, and then Linda's entire body seized up from a new eruption of pain, a second thrust of the knife blade, followed by a third, and at that moment she realized:

This would not end until she was dead.

The thin lips in the mask moved open and shut, panting, drooling strands of saliva. The eyes stayed wide open, unblinking, even as spots of blood sprayed the mask.

Linda had enough remaining strength for one final action. She removed her hand from where it had been clutching a wound. Her fingers were solid red, as if she had dipped them in paint. She brought the hand to her face and removed her glasses, allowing the terror scene to fall out of focus. The attacker, her blood, her apartment walls and furniture, framed family pictures, the knife's blade, the twisted mouth…it was all sucked away in a soft fog of color and light.

Linda Geesin's final sensation was the tip of the blade puncturing the skin beneath her eye, entering the socket, then tugging, as the man in the ski mask stated plainly, "I'm not sorry. I'm not sorry."

Chapter Fourteen

*L*et the victims begin.

After reading the final passage, Ellen pushed the notebook to the floor as if it had just burned her hands. She moved off the couch, staring at the red cover. The notebook had undergone a transformation. It couldn't be the same journal she had been reading every night for the past two weeks.

The voice no longer belonged to Charles, it had been taken over by someone sick and deranged. Yet the handwriting stayed identical to the previous pages. Ellen gasped for air.

Had she just read a murder confession?

Surely these words couldn't be true? They were merely that...just words.

Why would Charles talk about killing someone? Why would he pretend to be his brother Darren?

This couldn't be the same young man who had touched her heart with a sensitive examination of his life's pain and yearnings. This couldn't be the outcome of a haunted child's search for love and understanding. Why would someone who had witnessed the most horrible violence imaginable thrive on rekindling those fires?

Could Charles be schizophrenic? Was there an evil side she had not yet seen? Could Darren be a second personality? Did Charles have a brother at all?

Had she just spent a dinner date with both of them? Ellen shuddered. Exactly who was she dating, anyway? Was he dangerous? Had he really harmed someone? Or was it all a sick fantasy?

Why would he write those words?

Damn you, Charles! Ellen stumbled into the bathroom. She fell to the rug in front of the toilet. She convulsed with dry heaves, wanting to throw up, but nothing came out except for tears.

What is real?

Ellen felt consumed by an anxiety attack that bombarded her with punishing physical sensations she had not felt in years. She was sliding back into a horrible place. This was the worst betrayal in a history of betrayals: her father, then George Ravenwood, followed by her fiancé, Jeremy. And now Charles...the one individual she had believed she could count on because they had both suffered so terribly in childhood and spoke the same language...

She screamed out loud at Charles, the intensity of her voice echoing off the tiles and filling her ears. She considered calling the police. She considered calling Charles to confront him. Then she longed to hold him and kiss him and hear his reassurances that the notebook was not based in reality.

She moved away from the toilet, but couldn't go to bed. Her body buzzed and ached.

She had to return to the notebook and reread those final pages for clues. The whole thing *had* to be a mistake...a crazy rant...an imaginary persona...pure fiction and delusions.

Ellen returned to the notebook's final entry by Darren. Then she reread earlier passages and tried to reconcile the two voices. Were they both bogus?

It could just be a strange exercise, she told herself. The declaration of murder could be no more credible than the earlier intentions to commit suicide—the destructive contemplations had just turned outward. Perhaps these writings were nothing more than role play—imaginary characters for his unleashed anger. Could the whole thing be some complex psychological novel? First-person fiction about a man going over the edge?

Or was it true schizophrenia, captured in a diary? Had the Charles side of his brain purposely left the notebook behind to be discovered as evidence to punish Darren?

Ellen exhausted herself analyzing the possibilities. She returned the notebook to her desk drawer, shutting it with a loud slam. She dragged herself to bed.

The clock on her nightstand read two thirty-five a.m. She couldn't remember the last time she had been up this late. The street outside her window was unusually calm and dark, a foreign landscape. Ellen curled up tight under the covers. She knew she wouldn't sleep and waited for the morning light.

When she finally started drifting in and out of consciousness, the alarm sounded. She reset it for an hour later. On this morning, she would go straight to work. She had no desire to go to Pacific Coast Coffee. She simply didn't know what she would do if she ran into *him*.

Ellen remained awake on the bed, staring at the ceiling, head throbbing with confusion. She grew angry with herself for feeling so much passion for a man she barely knew in the flesh. She had instead fallen for words on paper, and now those words had turned on her.

When Ellen reported for work, punctual but lacking any energy, Peg looked into her eyes and beamed. "You look wiped. Late date night?"

"No," said Ellen.

Peg read the tension in Ellen's tone and quickly changed the subject. "Hey, you gotta check out the new display in the children's section. We made a tower of pop-up books."

To get through the morning, Ellen drank a cup of the Book Shelf's french roast, but didn't like it. As much as she tried, she couldn't force smiles for the customers.

After a few hours of watching Ellen drag herself around the store, Terri asked to speak with her and brought her into the back room. They stood in an area known as the morgue because it was filled with unsold magazines and mass-market paperbacks waiting for their covers to be torn off and returned to publishers for credit.

"Honey, are you okay?" asked Terri.

"I'm sorry," said Ellen. "I had a rough night. Personal issues. I didn't mean to let them get in the way of work."

"It's fine. We all have bad days. I just want you to know, if you need to talk, or you need help in some way, let me know. Sometimes I feel like a surrogate mother to you girls, and I don't like to see you 'out of place', if you know what I mean."

"I appreciate that," said Ellen. She felt an urge to hug Terri then and wished that Terri really was her mother.

"I know I gab a lot, but I'm a good listener, too. Okay?"

"Yes," said Ellen. "Thank you. I'm going to be all right. I just didn't sleep well. It helps being at work. Getting into my routine."

"If you need to leave, we'll get somebody to cover for you. We'll get someone from the next shift to come in early."

"No. I'm good. I'm fine. Really."

The door opened a crack. "Hey, Ellen!" cried Peg, poking her head into the room.

"We're having a private conversation," said Terri.

"I just wanted to tell her there's somebody here to see her." Peg quickly withdrew from the room.

Terri gave Ellen a pat on the shoulder. "Okay. I'm done. Get out there."

"Thanks, Terri."

Ellen left the back room. *Someone to see me?* She walked up the center aisle. She hoped it wasn't a customer with a problem.

As Ellen walked to the front of the store, she saw Charles talking to Peg.

Ellen nearly tripped over her own feet in an attempt to slow her pace. She wasn't ready for this...

Too late. Charles turned, saw her and smiled. "Hi, Ellen," he said softly.

"Hey," said Ellen. "Hi." She couldn't bring herself to say his name. She immediately felt self-conscious about her rumpled appearance. Her hair looked awful, she wore no makeup...

"So, is this your secret boyfriend?" said Peg with a grin. Ellen wanted to slug her.

Charles chuckled.

Peg continued, "I know Charles. I've sold him a lot of books. He's a total bookworm."

"I'm a readaholic," said Charles.

"He buys up all the new mysteries and thrillers," said Peg. "He likes murder and intrigue. I'd look out for him."

Charles chuckled again. Ellen didn't smile.

"Charles says you guys met at a coffee place," said Peg.

"Pacific Coast Coffee," said Ellen.

Peg faced Charles and teased him. "Hey, what's wrong with the coffee here?"

"You guys don't open until nine," responded Charles. "I need something earlier than that to get me going."

"I keep telling Terri we should open earlier," said Peg, animated, all her attention on Charles. Ellen thought, *Is she flirting with him?*

Standing side by side, Peg and Charles even looked cute together. Ellen felt a tug of jealousy. Charles wore his long coat, very handsome, with a hint of morning stubble on his finely chiseled cheeks.

Charles turned to Ellen. Ellen saw Peg's eyes remain on him.

He said, "The reason I came in… Well, it's twofold. There are some books I'm looking for, but I also wanted to see if you have any plans tonight."

Ellen spoke without a moment's thought. "No plans," she said, alarmed by her automatic response.

Peg stepped back, excusing herself. "I better go help customers," she said. "I'll leave you two alone."

Charles looked into Ellen's eyes. "I'd like to take you out tonight. Dinner, a movie or a club, whatever you'd like. I'd just like to see you sooner than Saturday."

"Sure," she said, and it was all happening too fast—it would have been so much easier to put him off over the phone, to stall for time, so she could think through this madness. But here, under the bright lights of the store, with his beautiful face looking at her, she could only offer compliance.

Everything was complicated in her head, yet she uttered simple, monosyllable responses.

Maybe I can just get him to dump me. I could probably do that without even trying.

After securing the dinner commitment, Charles began talking about books. He brought her into his favorite section of the store. He told her about his favorite authors of thrillers and mysteries, shared his favorite series characters, and lamented classics that had gone out of print. He loaded his arms with books that had titles like *Killer's Game*, *Bloody Mary*, *Abducted* and *Vengeance*.

"There's one more book I'm after," he said, leaving the mystery-thriller aisle. She followed him to the reference section, where he studied the spines of various books on writing.

He chose a fiction-writing handbook. Ellen felt a rush of relief. *He's a fiction writer. That crazy notebook, it must be fiction. A character. A creative writing exercise. Nothing more.*

She wanted to hug him right then and there. Her mood perked up.

He bought his books, and then she accompanied him into the enclosed area just inside the front entrance, between two sets of doors. Ellen could see Peg watching them from inside the store.

Charles gave Ellen a gentle kiss on the lips.

"I'll see you tonight," he said.

"Yes," she responded. "In just a few hours."

"I can't wait," he said, smiling.

She returned inside the store, feeling lighter and renewed.

Peg ambushed her. "Oh my God. He is so adorable. I am so happy for you. I've noticed him since the first time he set foot in the store. He's quiet, but really intelligent, really cool. Where are you guys going for dinner? Where are you going after? Now you're going to have to share details!"

Ellen spent the rest of the afternoon avoiding Peg. At four o'clock, the next shift arrived, including a woman named Molly. Molly was an older woman, divorced and humorless, who usually didn't talk much to Ellen or Peg, aside from grunts of hello and goodbye, as if their separate shifts made interaction irrelevant.

Today, however, she approached Ellen with an eager look in her eyes. She asked Ellen if she would consider exchanging shifts.

"You could sleep in, do whatever you want for most of the day," she said.

Ellen politely declined.

Peg came up after Molly had left. "Did she try to get you to switch shifts, too?"

"Yeah," said Ellen.

"I told her there was no way you'd do it, you need your evenings free. You've got a boyfriend now."

"Why is she so bent on working the day shift all of a sudden?"

"Because of what's been going on in the neighborhood."

"What's that?"

Peg looked incredulous. "Haven't you been following the news?"

Ellen shrugged. "A little. Not everything."

Peg lowered her voice as a customer browsed nearby. "Molly doesn't want to go back to her apartment late at night because of those murders. In the past three months, two girls have been stabbed to death. One of them was just around the block from her place, so she's totally freaked out. I told her to buy some mace. Or a gun." Peg broke out laughing. "Can you imagine Molly with a .38 special?"

All of the relief Ellen had felt when Charles picked up the fiction-writing handbook suddenly dissipated, replaced by a heavy renewed fear.

"Do they know who killed these girls?" Ellen asked. "Are there any clues?"

"Nothing," said Peg. "Just some maniac. Probably a crackhead. He killed one woman in a parking lot and another in her apartment. It's fucked up, but what can you do? It's part of living in the big city. You just gotta watch your back..."

Chapter Fifteen

Stepping into solid darkness, Ellen felt along the wall until she found the light switch. She snapped it on. A single light bulb, poking through cobwebs in the ceiling beams, exposed the utility room of her apartment building. The bulb's limited reach left huge patches of the room lost to shadows. She stepped forward cautiously, preparing herself for any scampering mice.

On her left, a succession of storage lockers belonging to tenants held everything from bicycles to old furniture to somebody's collection of empty jelly jars. On her right, the hulking boiler hummed valiantly to keep up with warming the winter chill.

Ellen advanced past the boiler to an ancient workbench against the wall. The surface was crowded with debris, presumably belonging to the building's maintenance man, Jerry, but probably predating him by decades.

On the counter, between cans of paint and a large vice, she found what she was looking for and remembered seeing here: a large hammer.

She picked it up by the handle—sticky, ick—and felt the weight of the head pull on her arm.

She couldn't imagine striking anybody with this hammer. Then again, she couldn't imagine Charles attacking her. But bringing this hammer into her apartment and hiding it within easy reach would make her feel a little safer for tonight's date.

It was insurance. She had gone online and researched, and what Peg said was true: two young women had been stabbed to death in the Lakeview neighborhood in the past eight weeks. While the thought of soft-spoken Charles actually harming anyone created a jarring picture in her mind, she just didn't know anything for sure. He had written about committing murder in a notebook. But why would a real killer write out a confession and leave it in a coffee shop? It didn't make sense.

She returned to her apartment. Just inside the door, she had several pairs of shoes lined up on a square mat: gym shoes, simple flats and a pair of knee-high black boots for snowy days. Ellen dropped the hammer into her left boot, where it disappeared from view. A convenient hiding place...unless it snowed.

There, happy? she asked herself. *At the end of the date, if he tries to invite himself in to kill you, just clobber him in the skull with the hammer, call the police and hand over the notebook. Ellen Gordon solves the case!*

She laughed inside, but also felt an overwhelming sadness. Over the course of the past couple of hours, she had prepared herself for breaking up with Charles. As much as she longed for him, the tone in his writing, truthful or not, had become too sinister and disturbing. They had connected on a level of pain and despair, but then he kept going, further than she could follow or accept.

Why does everything in my life end in disappointment and loss?

She prepared lines of dialogue that could bring their short relationship to a swift conclusion. But even as she rehearsed the words, she prepared herself to look her best, anxious to look beautiful in his eyes. She tried on five different outfits before finding the one that complemented her figure the best.

Her mind circled a variety of moods and she realized she hadn't felt this emotional—good or bad—in a long time, having successfully deadened her feelings in the wake of her childhood trauma and broken engagement.

If only I had the guts to confront Charles head on about the notebook, I could probably get a reasonable explanation. Maybe it's not even his work. Different people can have similar handwriting...

She gave herself a final look in the full-length mirror that hung on the back of her bedroom door. Was she dressy enough without overdoing it? Did the shoes match?

Ellen couldn't stop evaluating herself through his eyes.

———

He was punctual and greeted her with a kiss; right after hello, he leaned forward and met her lips with his, a sensation both firm and soft, delivering shudders under her skin. Before she could fully react, kissing him back as an active participant, he retreated with a big grin on his face. She felt breathless, as if she had just run ten laps.

He held out a wrapped gift.

"For you," he said.

"A present?" She stared at it, hands remaining at her sides. "Oh…that's not fair. I don't have a present for you."

"No, no. I know," he said. "It was spur-of-the-moment. I just saw it…and thought of you. Open it."

She accepted the gift and began tearing the blue wrapping paper.

He told her, "During dinner the other night, when we were talking about books and writing, you said you wanted to write poems and short stories. I just wanted to help that along. I think it's a wonderful ambition."

She unwrapped a handsome, cloth-bound notebook. Her own journal. It was so beautiful, she couldn't imagine marring it with her scribbly penmanship and uncertain prose.

"Thank you," she said, skimming a landscape of blank lined pages that awaited her profound thoughts.

"The best way to become a good, confident writer is to just write a lot," Charles said. "Keep it spontaneous and fresh. Don't worry about other people seeing it; just write for you. Write whatever comes to mind. You don't have to show it to anyone."

She studied his face and asked, "What I write in here…does it have to be true? Or can I make it up?"

He cocked his head. "Make it up?"

She felt a moment of fear and hated herself for blurting the question. But she had to search for clues in his response. He looked uncertain about her remark.

She said, "What I mean is, should I write about me, like a diary, or can I…invent things?"

Charles laughed then, which relieved her, because his face relaxed and lost any trace of suspicion. "Sure! Invent things. Tell secrets. Whatever you want, it's your journal."

"Maybe I'll write the great American novel," she said.

"Just don't use it for shopping lists and phone numbers. It's not that kind of notebook."

All this talk about notebooks and journals was making her dizzy. Or was she dizzy from hunger? She put the gift aside on a chair. "We should probably go," she said. "What time are the dinner reservations?"

He glanced at his watch. "Seven thirty. We have just enough time to grab a cab." He turned toward the door, and in doing so, accidentally kicked over one of her boots.

The boot toppled and the handle of a hammer slid out.

In a shot of panic, Ellen jumped in front of Charles to keep his attention off the floor. She touched his arm. "You go ahead. I'll grab my coat and be right with you."

"All right. You kicking me out?"

"Of course not." She gave him a quick kiss and pointed him to the door.

"I'll go start looking for a cab," he said.

After he left, Ellen put the hammer back in the boot. She grabbed her long winter coat out of the closet.

How am I going to enjoy this dinner if I'm a nervous wreck?

———

She drank two glasses of Zinfandel before her entrée arrived, and that helped settle her down. It also increased her longing for Charles, setting free her feelings of passion and excitement all over again.

Louie's was a classic steak house, more formal and romantic than their first-date restaurant, with chamber music playing in overhead speakers and older, dignified waiters in white shirts with black vests.

Charles ordered his steak rare and then joked to the waiter, "But not too bloody."

Ellen forced a smile and took a long sip of wine.

For dinner conversation, she had three topics that would help her determine if Charles could be linked to the murders. The trick was finding ways to integrate the topics without sounding probing.

Item number one: where did Charles live? He had mentioned a high-rise condominium, but not pinpointed a location. For both dates, he had taken a cab to her building, so she knew he didn't live within walking distance.

Immediately after work, Ellen had spent an hour on her home PC researching the two murders in the Lakeview neighborhood. She knew the precise locations where the killings had taken place. Did Charles live anywhere near where the victims were discovered?

After the main course had arrived and Ellen had taken several bites of her filet, she said, "This is really good. Good choice. Do you come here a lot?"

"Only on special occasions."

"Do you live near here?"

"No. Not really. Sort of."

"Are you closer to downtown?"

"You could say that." His eyes glanced around the room, as if searching out a distraction.

"So where do you live, anyway?"

"The Gold Coast."

"Really? Where?" The Gold Coast was an exclusive, upscale community near the lakefront, close to downtown. She was impressed.

"On LaSalle Street."

"I have a friend who lives in that area," Ellen lied. "Which building are you in?"

"It's the big one."

"Which big one?"

"On the corner of Lincoln and LaSalle."

"Lincoln and LaSalle?"

"Yes, the big one right on the corner."

Based on his response, Ellen felt satisfied that Charles lived a good distance from the murders. She was confident enough to advance to her next round of *fact or fiction*: the murder of Charles's mother at the hands of his father.

"My mom called me today," Ellen said, lie number two. Her mother never called anymore, but Ellen was carefully crafting a segue. "She wants me to come out and visit, like I can just leave work and everything at the drop of a hat. She lives downstate, near Springfield. I'm glad she doesn't live so close that she could just drop by whenever she wanted, because she would if she could. How about you? Do your parents live around here?"

"No, they're in Arizona," said Charles, matter-of-fact, biting into a pink chunk of meat.

"Both of them?"

"Yeah. My dad retired about eight years ago. He hated the Chicago winters. He has arthritis—the dampness and everything really bothered him." He spoke in a bland tone.

Two for two, thought Ellen. *Of course, he could be making it up...but it really doesn't sound like it. He didn't even hesitate when I mentioned his parents. If his father really hacked his mother to death with a butcher knife, wouldn't there be some faint reaction? A cringe? An awkward pause?*

The notebook was seeming more like melodramatic fiction all the time.

"What did your dad do before he retired?" she asked.

"He worked as a salesman for a drug company."

Ellen nodded, chewing her food, satisfied with the response until she realized that Charles had just contradicted himself.

During their previous date, hadn't he told her that his father worked in insurance?

Maybe he had worked both jobs over the course of his career? Or was Charles spinning fiction?

Ellen jumped to question number three. She meant to ask, "Do you have any sisters or brothers?"

She got as far as "Do—"

Charles interrupted her. "Have you ever been to the Cave?"

"The Cave?"

"It's a new club."

"No. I haven't..." She hadn't been out to many clubs, even though her neighborhood was filled with them. Her dating dry spell had effectively grounded her. Sometimes she heard Peg talking about various night spots, but she couldn't remember Peg ever talking about the Cave.

"Good. Then it'll be a new experience," said Charles. "I'd like to take you there after dinner, for drinks, if you don't mind. It's a pretty cool hangout. It's designed like an underground cave, with fake stone walls and passageways that take you all over, into different rooms. It's a labyrinth. I know all the secret ways to get around. Sometimes people get so drunk they can't find their way out."

"Oh, great," said Ellen. "That'll be me."

"I'll be your guide," said Charles, reaching across the table for her hand. She felt his touch and wanted badly to pull him close. He said, "With me, you won't have anything to worry about."

Chapter Sixteen

Charles took Ellen's hand and held it firmly as they navigated the busy sidewalks and street intersections. They crossed five blocks and the nightlife activity diminished with each new curb. Restaurants and storefronts vanished, replaced with silent manufacturers and bland office buildings. The traffic became sparse and their path lost its streetlamp shine.

"Where is this place?" asked Ellen, huddling closer to Charles to block the cold gusts of air.

Charles stopped walking. She bumped into him. He faced a long, dark alley.

"Here," he said.

"You're kidding."

"It's at the end of the alley."

"I don't see anything."

"Of course not. It would be totally uncool if it drew attention to itself. It's not a frat bar."

"I don't even see a sign."

"People know where to find it. That's what gives it an 'insider' feel. C'mon."

Charles kept their hands locked, tugging on her arm. He advanced into the darkness. She followed, feeling a rush of fear. If he tried anything, could she scream loud enough to alert somebody? Could she break his grasp and run into the street?

"Charles, I don't know…"

He didn't respond.

The alley had potholes and cracked concrete. She fought to keep up with him and avoid stumbling.

Once they were about fifty feet into the alley, out of view from the street, Charles stopped. Wordlessly, he reached for something with his free hand, digging into his coat…

Is he getting his knife?

Ellen yanked her hand free, throwing Charles off balance.

He stared back at her in surprise. He held his wallet.

"What's the matter?" he said. "I need my ID. You'll need your ID, too."

"Right," she said. At that moment a large steel door swung open next to them, unleashing the loud, crashing beats of industrial music. Two skinny, pale young men emerged, wearing black trench coats. One of them glanced at Ellen. He wore eyeliner.

Charles motioned for Ellen to follow him inside. "C'mon. Let's enter the Cave."

They stepped through the door together. It slammed shut behind them. A burly man with a shaved head checked their IDs with a tiny flashlight. A bony woman next to him collected the cover charge. She wore a black minidress, sleeveless black blouse, black lipstick and a small hat with a mourning veil. As she took the money from Charles, her eyes stared at Ellen. Either she was attracted to Ellen or simply amused by Ellen's nervous expression. "Have a good time, sweetie," she said.

Ellen and Charles went down a tunnel. The walls seemed to throb from the music. They turned a corner and spilled into a large, multi-level dance bar that looked carved out of rock. An eruption of people jammed the floor and overhead catwalks, bathed in black light.

Ellen noticed her white blouse and pearls glowing purple and felt self-conscious, exposed for being unhip.

Charles was shouting at her and she could barely hear him. On the third try, she heard "…go to the bar and get some drinks."

She nodded yes.

They had to snake through the dance floor to get to the other side. Ellen dodged elbows and feet, jostled by the crowd. She noticed that Charles drew hungry looks from many of the women and even a few men. He was handsome in a dark way that this crowd apparently found appealing.

On a shelf above the bar, a lineup of bleached animal skulls stared down at them. Charles ordered drinks. As they waited, a woman standing next to Charles started a conversation with him. She had short, copper-colored hair and wore a cat collar with studs. Ellen couldn't hear their words, but forced herself closer to Charles so the woman could see that he was taken.

Charles handed Ellen a plastic cup filled with green liquid. It was very full, so she took a sip. The strong taste jerked her head back. She felt an immediate warmth rising inside.

She heard a hissing sound. She turned to see fog from dry ice pour onto the dance floor. She watched an entangled couple clad in black kissing and groping before they became lost in the rolling fog. Large video monitors hung from the ceiling, displaying a montage of horror and cult movie clips.

Charles stepped in front of her, taking a large swallow of his green drink. He shouted something that she couldn't hear. She shrugged, so he moved closer and reduced his words to, "Follow me."

Charles circled the perimeter of the dance floor and Ellen followed close behind. He slipped into a passageway that looked like a crack in the wall. She accompanied him into a network of tunnels that led to various pockets of space, private compartments that held couches, overstuffed chairs, tables and occasional video monitors. When he found a small empty room, he eagerly occupied it.

"We've got some privacy," he said. "It's easier to talk. We won't have to lip read."

"I feel out of place without my nose ring," she said.

"You'd look good with a nose ring," he said, and she couldn't tell if he was kidding.

"Do you come to this place a lot?" she asked.

"No," he said. "Just when I want to do something a little different, when I want to explore the dark side." He took another swallow of his green drink.

"You certainly know all the trails through here."

"It's not that complicated. It only seems that way because it's so dark."

"Do you have a map to the bathroom?" Her plastic cup was empty and she really had to go.

"You'll have to go out the way we came," he said, and he offered a zigzag of directions.

She promised to return in a couple of minutes.

Ellen wound her way back to the dance floor, walking in stops and starts as the path offered split trails and alternate routes. The drinks at dinner, followed by the green thing here, didn't help. Ellen finally asked another girl the way to the bathroom. The girl looked underage. She wore long black gloves and a skirt that stopped mid-thigh.

"That's where I'm going. Follow me."

In the women's room, Ellen encountered decent lighting for the first time and had a chance to check herself out in the mirror.

She was definitely dressed all wrong for this crowd. They wore their darkness on the outside.

My darkness is all on the inside, she thought. *And that's where I want it to stay.*

She washed her hands, played with her hair for a moment, and then headed back to find Charles.

She became hopelessly lost.

Ellen re-entered the web of tunnels and small rooms. Everything looked the same—and nothing looked familiar. She proceeded deeper into the passageways, the thumping music from the dance floor fading behind her. She circled past a threesome of staring, black-clad goths and feared they could sense her growing anxiety. The farther she went, the colder and darker the faces around her became.

Passing one of the cubbyholes, Ellen heard a woman in torn fishnet stockings tell her friend, "I heard a girl was raped in here last month…"

Ellen turned a corner and faced a stone wall. She retreated, found another tunnel, and stepped into a space where two shadowy figures slid up and down against one another, hands underneath each other's clothing. She had to squint to identify the pairing. Man-woman, man-man, woman-woman? It was anyone's guess.

Ellen headed back in another direction, following another path. She thought about Charles waiting for her, growing impatient and irritated. She picked up her pace…

…and crashed into a large, broad-chested man with wild, frizzy hair. He scowled and she quickly spun away from him. She ran on, entering another corridor.

Ellen heard laughter and encountered several more dark figures. One of them called out, "Nice outfit, Grandma."

A second voice shouted, "Come party with us."

Ellen hurried away from them, heading into another passageway, which led to another dead end, forcing her to turn left, then make a fast right…

…slamming into Charles. He broke out laughing. "There you are!"

"I got lost…" she started to say, and then his arms closed around her, tightening his hold. She welcomed the embrace, its rugged warmth, and leaned up to kiss him. He returned the kiss, lips rolling against hers, and she dug her fingers into his shoulders. She shut her eyes, completely succumbing to the dark, all things reduced to the senses he brought to life with his touch, smell and lips.

When they came apart, he said, "You must have really missed me."

She smiled, couldn't come up with any words and looked away shyly.

"Do you want another drink?" he asked.

"Actually…" she said.

He could read it off her face. "You want to go someplace else?"

"Sure," she eagerly accepted.

"Well, I picked this place. You pick the next place. Anywhere you want to go."

She thought about it. She didn't really have a favorite club or hangout. But she didn't want this evening to end. It was still early…

She blurted out the only bar in the area that she knew, Dartz, because it was close to her apartment and she had gone there a few times before with friends. The familiarity would be comforting, even if she was indifferent to the environment and its clientele.

"Dartz," said Charles. "Sure. I've been there. We can go there. It's not far."

"Unless you want to stay here…" she offered.

"No," he said. "Let's keep moving." Then he said, "Before we go…" and leaned in and kissed her again. It began as a short kiss, but she grabbed him and held him in place, capturing the moment.

Chapter Seventeen

Within her first five minutes inside Dartz, Ellen felt a thrill. It was the same old bar, but she felt altogether different. She had stepped across a boundary. Instead of being another lonely single hanging along the rim of an urban meat market, she had become one of the people she used to watch with envy: a confident woman attached to a good-looking man. She felt taller, lighter. She could see young, upwardly mobile women stealing glances at Charles—and their eyes traveling to the date at his side. *He's taken.*

For a moment, Ellen had an out-of-body experience. She observed Charles and herself from somewhere across the room. She watched through the eyes of her old self, shoulders slumped, afraid to make conversation, uncertain about her body and face and personality. That was the former Ellen: hungry for human contact, yet frightened by it, anxiety level high from the contradiction.

But entering tonight, here and now, this was the new Ellen.

Dartz was crowded, but with Charles at her side, she could cut through the walls of bodies in her path. People wouldn't move for her, perhaps, but they did move for *them.* The claustrophobia she often felt in crowds melted away.

Compared to the Cave, Dartz had more light and color, spread through a simple, sprawling layout. Muted plasma TV screens showed a hockey game. High-energy pop hits rained down from elevated speakers, providing a steady pulse that didn't interfere with conversations. Voices came at her from every angle, entangled threads of chatter without beginning or end, punctuated with laughter and shouts.

Charles led her to an open space near a corridor that connected the bar to a restaurant. He asked her what she wanted to drink.

"A beer," she said.

"It's a micro-brewery. I think we can do that. Anything in particular?"

"No," she said. "Surprise me."

"I'm full of surprises," he said.

"I know."

"Don't disappear on me. I'll be right back."

"I'm not going anywhere."

She watched him move through openings in the crowd until he vanished from view. Then she turned her sights on the faces around her. She wondered if she'd find Peg—it was one of her favorite hangouts. Peg was not shy about describing the occasional one-night stands she picked up here. In her storytelling, she turned the men into cartoons, describing their oafishness and idiosyncrasies in hilarious detail, concluding her anecdotes with "I was shitfaced. I'll never see him again because I'll never recognize him again."

Ellen thought about Peg's open admiration of Charles. Earlier in the day, Peg had told her, "I go fishing every weekend, hitting every bar in the city, while you stay at home, reading books, doing nothing, and you land the big prize. There's no justice."

Peg was kidding. Sort of.

"Ellen! What are you doing here?"

Ellen turned, searching out the source of the voice. She scanned the people around her.

Jeremy stepped through the crowd.

For a moment, she locked up. It was like two worlds colliding. Jeremy didn't compute. He was part of another life.

She was shocked to find her newfound happiness and confidence melting away just from his presence. He reminded her of everything that was wrong.

"What's with the big hair?" he laughed.

All at once, she felt self-conscious.

He said, "Makeup...fancy clothes. Lip gloss. Jeez, I almost didn't recognize you."

"Hi, Jeremy," she said flatly. "What are you up to?"

"I'm in the back room with C.J., playing pool."

C.J. was one of Jeremy's dorkier friends—he ate nothing but fast food and sold bootleg DVDs of Japanese martial arts films out of his apartment.

"Sounds like a blast," she said, an unusual blurt of sarcasm for her, but it felt good—as if she was meeting him on his level of snideness instead of cowed by it.

"C.J. says he saw you working at a bookstore." His voice was slurred.

"The Book Shelf? Yes."

"Still into books. Nothing new there. What else have you been up to? Living a life of excitement?"

"More exciting than playing pool with C.J."

Jeremy's eyes narrowed, startled by her tone. "What? You've got an attitude now?"

"I guess yours must have rubbed off on me."

"Lighten up. You know me. I kid around. I don't mean anything."

"Like when you said we were going to get married?"

"You're not still mad about that?"

"No," she said, which was honest. She had to bite her tongue because she wanted to add, "Thank God it didn't happen."

"You need more meat on your bones," said Jeremy. He poked her arm. "It looks like you got AIDS or anorexia or something. I'm not saying you should get fat, but Jesus…"

"Thank you, Dr. Jeremy," she said, and her gaze left him and scanned the crowd for Charles.

"So are you here all by yourself? I gotta tell you, nobody's going to pick you up if you hide back here looking at the floor."

"I'm here with a date," she said firmly, looking back at him, square in the face. *I hope Charles gets here soon so you can see how good looking and smooth he is. He's way out of your league.*

"A date?" Jeremy said, perplexed, as if she had just told him a flying saucer had landed.

Ellen felt her back and neck tense up. "I don't like that tone," she said. "I never liked it. All the time we were dating, you always used such a condescending tone with me."

"Oh, what, you're going to dredge up stuff from the ancient past?"

"I mean it."

"You liked it when I treated you that way. You just won't admit it. You liked playing the soft, passive little girl that other people tell what to do. That's your shtick."

"My shtick?"

"So who's this guy? Does he work at the bookstore? Is he a nerd?"

"Why don't you leave me alone, Jeremy?"

"You don't want me to leave you alone. You still have a thing for me. I can tell."

"Hah. You are way off."

"Hey…" He moved in closer. She tried backing up, but her shoulder blades touched the wall. "Hey, Ellen," he said, reaching up and touching her hair. "Remember that time we came here on a date? It was summer, and the rooftop deck was open. You could see the lights of the skyline. We found that area where no one could see us…"

She remembered. He had been drunk and grabbed her breast—hard, not gently—and started dry-humping her until her lack of response pissed him off.

Jeremy's eyes came alive, as if it was a highlight of their relationship. Perhaps he only remembered his erection, and not her pleading, "Stop it, there are people up here. You're hurting me…"

Jeremy leaned in closer. She could smell the beer on his breath and see the sloppy way his mouth moved when he was drunk. "Let's go to my place. I have rubbers. It's okay. I think it's the big hair thing. It turns me on."

She turned her head away from him. "I think it's the beer. You're drunk, Jeremy."

His face hardened. "Bullshit. A couple of beers does not make me drunk. You, maybe, because you're a friggin' skeleton."

"You're drunk. I know what you're like when you're drunk. I know how you sound, how you behave. I wish I could hold up a mirror so you could see yourself."

"So are you screwing this new guy?"

"Gee, that came out of nowhere."

Jeremy echoed her words back at her, scrunching up his features, pinched and mean, spitting out the remarks in a grotesque sing-song voice. "'Gee, that came out of nowhere.'"

"I've had enough."

"I'll bet he's *not* screwing you. Or if he is, you're so goddamned frigid, it's like screwing a board."

"You ever heard of foreplay, Jeremy?"

"Fuck you," he spat, and Evil Jeremy was back, the person she hated, the person who had hurt her a thousand times, who wanted nothing more than to belittle her and cut her down and then plead for forgiveness when he got horny. It made her sick.

She tried to squirm away. "Leave me alone. Go back to your pool game."

"This is public property. I can stand here. I can talk to you. Freedom of speech!" Slivers of spittle shot from his lips. He looked and sounded ridiculous. He moved closer to her, toe to toe.

"Jeremy, I mean it—!"

"*Move away from her!*" Charles appeared, gripping two glasses of beer, jabbing his elbow into Jeremy's chest. Jeremy stumbled to one side.

"What the fuck, buddy!" shouted Jeremy. "You don't touch me." He sprung back at Charles and shoved him.

The beers splashed back on Charles. As soon as the beer hit his shirt, Charles threw both glasses to the floor and charged Jeremy.

The two men started to tangle, clutching at each other's shirts. A large bouncer in a white Dartz shirt jumped into the fray, pulling them apart.

"This asshole—!" started Jeremy, panting.

The bouncer cut him off. "I don't give a shit. You don't fight in here. Take it outside. I don't care what you do out there, but you will not fight in here."

Charles's hands remained clenched into fists. "Fine. Outside then."

Jeremy hesitated, recognizing that Charles was taller and thicker. But a fire still burned behind his eyes—no doubt fueled by alcohol. "Okay. You want it, you got it. You don't know what you're getting into, fella. I've got a fucking black belt."

Ellen seriously doubted this claim, unless a black belt could be earned simply by watching a lot of bad karate movies.

"This is stupid," said Ellen, "Let's just leave." She moved to Charles's side, wrapping an arm around his waist to pull him with her. She couldn't budge him.

"Who is this creep?" asked Charles.

"He's an old…acquaintance." Ellen didn't even want to honor Jeremy with the word "boyfriend."

"That's right, fucker," said Jeremy. "So why don't you cool it before you get hurt in front of your bitch."

Charles pulled away from Ellen and stepped toward Jeremy. He jabbed a finger at him, nearly striking him between the eyes. "You, me, outside, *now*. RIGHT NOW!"

Ellen shuddered. Charles's voice had reached a volume and fierceness she had never heard before. Faces in the crowd stared at them from every direction. She said, "Please, Charles…"

"Let's do it," said Jeremy to Charles.

The two men moved toward the exit. Patrons stumbled out of their path, recognizing the intensity in their eyes. Ellen followed, falling behind. Her heart raced madly. She felt a choking in her throat, as if she was about to erupt in a sob.

"Charles, don't!" she cried out. Her voice was lost in the rising buzz surrounding the impending brawl.

When Ellen made it outside, she had to push past a layer of people who had already started gathering to watch the confrontation. She heard Jeremy shouting in a drunken voice that resembled that of a bratty child, "You don't fucking touch me. You don't touch me!"

Then she saw the two of them on the sidewalk. Jeremy had already started to adopt some clumsy kung fu posturing that looked more fake than genuine. Charles was undeterred and struck the first blow, delivering a punch to Jeremy's cheek. Jeremy responded with a punch aimed for Charles's face, but caught him in the neck instead, which was probably worse. From there, the swinging and punching erupted from both sides, a combination of hits and misses, and the whole scene became so primitive and ugly that Ellen wanted to turn away, but she couldn't remove her gaze from the crashing bodies.

In less than a minute, Jeremy was doubled up from a sequence of hammering blows that caused some of the bystanders to gasp just from the sound of the impact. Jeremy attempted to charge back at Charles, arms outstretched to grab him. Charles turned the momentum back on his attacker, slamming him into the brick wall adjacent to a window, where a growing number of faces had collected to watch from inside the bar.

As Jeremy crumpled, Charles grew fiercer, transforming into someone else, raging and animalistic. He continued punching Jeremy until Jeremy had fallen too low to reach, and then he began kicking him savagely in the stomach and head, and somewhere a cut must have opened, because Jeremy's face became striped with blood. It pooled in his ear and when he cried out, Ellen could see his reddened teeth and blood-smeared mouth, a sight so awful that she screamed, "*Stop it, STOP IT!*" louder than anything she had ever screamed before in her life.

The crowd, equally stunned by Charles's ferocious outburst, stumbled back to give him extra space, as if he was just wild enough to turn on a random onlooker next. Jeremy spit blood on the sidewalk and muttered unconvincingly through swollen lips, "Asshole, I'll fucking kill you." One bystander was brave enough—or drunk enough—to snap a few pictures with his cell phone.

A police siren tore into the night.

Charles gave Jeremy one more kick to the head, causing him to expel a large grunt. Then Charles turned to Ellen, eyes wide as if surprised by his own actions, and said, "Let's get out of here."

Ellen found herself running to keep up with Charles as he hurried away from Dartz in long, swift strides. The police siren grew louder and Charles turned the first corner he reached.

"C'mon, c'mon," he said to Ellen. "I don't want to get arrested because of that idiot."

They continued for about half a block, and then Ellen saw another police car, lit up, heading in their direction.

"In here," said Charles, ducking into an alley.

She followed him. He flattened against the wall of a building. As she got close, he reached out and grabbed her wrist, pulling her into him.

They watched the alley turn colors from the pulsing lights of the police car. It roared past them. They remained still. She could feel Charles's heavy breathing. "We're okay," he said.

She looked up at him in the dark and at that moment felt safe and protected against anything and everything that could ever hurt her. He looked down at her face, and she slid up against him and kissed his lips. He grasped her around the waist and kissed back, forcefully.

"I'm sorry…" he said, muffled.

"No," she said. "Thank you." As horrible as it had been to witness the fight, she now felt strangely exhilarated by it. She realized how deeply she resented Jeremy, how he reminded her of the worst in herself, how he brought out her bad qualities and insecurities, and beating him back—*really* beating him back—felt like breaking free, out of some shell. She was experiencing life now, tasting it, smelling it, feeling it, like never before, in new dimensions and colors.

Old Ellen had been knocked out of play tonight. Now there was only new Ellen and her future.

"The police won't find us…at my place," she offered.

She could feel his response—the smile that grew across his lips as he continued to kiss her in the shadows, against the brick.

They stumbled into her apartment together, entangled like a single entity. It took several tries to close the door behind them without interfering with their passion. He clutched both of her hands in his, slapping them against a wall, bodies rough, lips tender, kisses rolling like small waves. She felt his broad chest press against her. She rippled with excitement, turned on beyond anything she had ever known. Sounds of pleasure erupted from deep within her, foreign to her ears. Her entire body unwound, weightless and drifting on a new plane.

He controlled the choreography, but she was an eager participant. She answered his cues. She followed his moves. He expressed his pleasure.

In the bedroom, she turned out the lights. He turned them back on. He unbuttoned her blouse. She blushed.

She still felt self-conscious about her body, an insecurity she had carried since puberty.

"You're beautiful," he told her definitively. He removed all her feelings of doubt with the delicious and loving way he traced her skin with his fingertips, leaving kisses along the way.

On the bed, he told her to relax. "I'm trying to," she said, opening up to him. "It's just been…a long time."

She realized he probably didn't understand her comment. She didn't mean it had been a long time since she last had sex…although the number of months was in double digits.

No, what she meant was that it had been a long time, so very long…since she had relaxed.

She felt layers of her past, ugly tensions, lift off and float to the heavens, and the sensation made her want to cry, a happy, relieved crying.

He stripped down and his body was shaped with perfectly placed angles and curves, something out of a classic figure drawing, scientific and pure, rendered offbeat by a skull tattoo on his round, muscular shoulder.

He kissed her nipples. He touched her down below, gently gaining acceptance, something she could feel but not imagine. She sucked on his thumb, and then on his fingers. She saw the scrapes and stains of blood on his knuckles. Jeremy's blood. She realized she was licking Jeremy's spilled blood and it made her tingle with sensation.

Fuck you, Jeremy. Fuck you, George. Fuck every man who ever fucked with me.

She recalled the fists pounding Jeremy to the pavement. She closed her eyes tight, tighter, and imagined an enormous letting go, a release, like a rolling flood.

Ellen felt tremors she had never felt before, passion and excitement pouring forth that she had never known lived inside her. The realization took over that she was nearly thirty and had never truly made love. She had been molested, she had been fucked—but those things were far away, they were nothing events, because this was the real thing, a warm touch from another unlike anything else, something that she had read about in a million books and written off as fiction, but never experienced or believed in, until right now, living deep inside the moment.

Chapter Eighteen

She slept deeply, physically exhausted, emotionally cleansed, naked and freed under the sheets. He held on with both arms pressed warm around her. When she awoke, the morning brought fresh stimulation, taking her back to early childhood, when each day felt epic with wonder and uncharted territory. Surely this wasn't the same apartment where she had awoken thousands of mornings before. These weren't the same walls that had suffocated her with narrow possibilities, lockstep routine and a low, omnipresent layer of dread. Charles gave her a new lease on life. Everything came into focus now in ways that displayed previously hidden richness.

For twenty minutes, she didn't move. She didn't want to wake him. She wanted to lie in bed and feel him against her, the softness of his breathing on her neck, the strength of his arms and legs. She wanted to absorb it all, recharging herself through his energy.

When he did awake, she pretended to wake with him. He looked at her and smiled.

"You probably need to get to work," he said.

"So do you," she said.

"That's right."

But neither one of them moved. Finally, he pulled her closer and kissed her.

Just when it appeared that they were headed for another session of lovemaking, he pulled back. "If we get started, we'll never get to where we need to go. Let's leave something for tonight. Tonight is good?"

"Tonight is very good," she said.

He stepped out of bed, feet hitting the floor firmly. He reached down for some clothes and started to get dressed.

He pulled on his pants, then looked around and laughed.

"What?" she said, sitting up.

"My clothes are in a trail."

She grinned. "Yes, I remember."

He left the bedroom, calling out his locations as he followed his clothing. "Hallway…living room…couch…behind the TV set?"

"You made that one up," she called after him.

His voice continued from the other room. "This bookcase is massive! Do you think you have enough books?"

"Never!" she said, sitting up cross-legged under the sheets.

"How did you even get this in here?"

"Piece by piece. I paid a guy to assemble it."

"This bookcase is taller than I am."

"Jealous?" she said.

"Possibly." Then he said, "Hey, if I wanted to call you at work, do you have a cell phone?"

"No."

"No?"

"I'm in the dark ages, I know."

"Can I call you at the bookstore? Will they get mad if you receive personal calls?"

"Not from you. You're a customer."

"That's right. I've spent a lot of dough in that place. What's the number? I'll write it down."

She started reciting the Book Shelf's phone number but he called out for her to wait a second so he could find paper and a pen.

Then there was a long silence.

She figured he wasn't finding what he needed, so she threw back the sheets, stepping out of bed. "I'll get it." As she was putting on her robe, Charles entered the bedroom.

He held the red notebook.

"This was in your drawer," he said.

She froze in shock, one arm halfway into a sleeve of her robe.

His eyes studied her. His face had lost its warmth and was becoming stoic and hard.

"I..." she said. She didn't know what to tell him.

"I opened your desk drawer to look for a pen, and I find *my notebook*. Why do you have this?"

"I found it," she said. It came out feeble. Her words struggled past the tightness in her throat.

He stepped closer, shirtless, chest heaving. "How long have you had this?"

"A couple of weeks, I guess."

"*A couple of weeks?*"

She finished pulling on her robe, looking at it so she wouldn't have to look at him. She tied the sash, hands trembling. "Please don't yell..."

"I'm not yelling. I'm asking—I'm pissed off—you knew this belonged to me?"

She nodded.

"This is my personal property, Ellen. It doesn't belong to you."

"I found it on a chair at the coffeehouse."

"God, that's where I thought I lost it. It must have been weeks ago, right?"

She nodded again.

"I've been freaking out," he said. "I've been waiting for this to turn up. I've been going crazy."

"I was going to give it back to you."

"When?"

"I don't know."

"Never?"

"No."

"You knew it belonged to me and you had no intention of telling me?"

"No, that's not true."

"Do you know how this makes me feel?" His voice simmered. "I thought we had a real relationship. What's a relationship without trust? You've had my notebook this entire time and you never said a word."

His tone sharpened, turning louder. "This is so messed up. What's wrong with you? Why the hell wouldn't you tell me you had this?"

"*Because I was scared!*" she shouted back at him.

He became speechless. He stared into her eyes. He stepped closer.

"Scared?" he said.

"I read it."

"You read it. And…"

"Well, you know…"

"No. I don't know. You tell me."

"I don't want to…" Ellen felt dizzy. Everything was falling apart around her. She wanted to shrink to the floor. She had woken up ecstatically happy…now this. She wanted to curl up and shield herself from the pounding waves of anxiety.

Standing before her, Charles appeared like a different person. His face had toughened, his mouth twisted in an angry scowl. All warmth and closeness had drained out of him.

"Tell me, Ellen," he spoke plainly. "What's bothering you about the notebook?'

"It says…maybe you hurt or killed someone."

His head jerked back and he let out a loud, harsh laugh.

She watched his reaction, confused.

"Ellen, sweetie…" he said. "You think…everything in that notebook is real?"

"I don't know," she said, swallowing back tears, feeling weakness in her knees. "It starts out one way…and then it becomes Darren and talks about a murder…"

"Do you think I'm Darren?"

"Sometimes, maybe. I don't know."

"I see. I'm Darren sometimes? Do you see a split personality?"

"It's in the notebook."

Charles said, "If I have a split personality, then where is my other half? Where's Darren?" He called out, "Darren, where are you? Hello? Darren, are you hiding in the closet?"

"Stop making fun of me."

"Listen, Ellen. These are characters. It's fiction. You work in a bookstore, for Christ's sake. Surely you know about the land of make-believe."

"It didn't read that way..."

"Sometimes you're so naïve." He sighed. "It's endearing, but it's also frustrating."

"Why would you make all that up?"

"Ellen, you know I read a lot of crime books. Mysteries and thrillers. You know I write. This notebook...I'm getting into the mind of a schizophrenic killer. The psychology, the back history. That's what authors do. They invent characters to see where they go. This is just...it's not even intended for an audience. It's stream-of-consciousness. It's an exercise. I'm exploring the dark side—like going to the Cave. The people in that notebook interest me. What makes a man reach that turning point where he becomes a murderer? What goes on in his brain? What happened to him as a child? It's like method acting, getting into character."

"Why would you want to be that character?"

"Why is any of this stuff so popular? Look at your bestseller rack. It's escapism."

"So all those stories about your childhood..."

"It's not *my* childhood."

"...you made it all up?"

"Of course."

"But the feelings you wrote about..." she said and stopped.

Charles seemed to fragment in front of her. If he wasn't the voice in the journal...then had she fallen in love with someone who didn't exist? Was she really in love with this strange man who had taken her to that weird Cave bar and been so distant and uncommunicative on their dates? Or was she drawn to the sensitive, brooding character who lived only on notebook paper...with no flesh and blood behind it?

"So you think I'm a killer?" he said.

"You nearly killed someone last night."

"That jerk in the bar? No. I *could* have killed him. But I don't go around killing people. There are laws."

"There have been murders in Lakeview."

"Now I'm responsible for every dead body in Chicago?"

"What about your parents?"

"I told you before, my parents live in Arizona."

"You didn't walk in on..."

He laughed again. "My father stabbing my mother to death? No. It's melodrama. It's the turning point for the character I invented."

"But you said your dad worked in insurance, and then you said he was a salesman for a drug company..."

He frowned. "Oh. So I'm a liar, and I'm just covering up for the fact that everything in the notebook is true, and I'm a maniac. Thanks, Ellen. I really appreciate your high opinion of me."

"That's not what I meant..."

"Let me ask you this, Ellen," he said. "If you think I'm the character in this notebook, then what the hell are you doing dating me, letting me sleep in your bed? I mean, I could cut your throat in the middle of the night. Doesn't that scare you?"

She couldn't respond.

He continued, "Or...I don't know, maybe it turns you on. Maybe your life is so boring that the only way you can get excited is if you imagine yourself rubbing up against a psychopathic killer."

His tone stung—it was Jeremy, it was George Ravenwood—it was the harsh condescension all over again.

She wouldn't allow it.

"You have to go," she said. She looked at the floor. She had nothing else to say. She didn't want to see his eyes anymore or hear his voice distorted by meanness.

"Okay," he said. He clutched the red notebook so tightly that it bent in his large hand. "I'll go, if that's what you want. That's what you want?"

She nodded.

He gathered his things, finished getting dressed, and left.

As soon as the door shut, leaving her in isolation, dropped back at square one, she knew she had made a mistake.

She clamped a hand over her mouth but couldn't control the sobs. Confusion spun inside her head. Had she ruined a rare chance at happiness? She didn't know what was real anymore, beginning with her feelings for Charles.

It couldn't end like this, not so fast with so many unanswered questions.

———

Before reporting to work at the Book Shelf, she stopped in Pacific Coast Coffee, armed with an apology she had rehearsed in the shower, during breakfast and while getting dressed.

However, Charles never turned up. She watched the coffeehouse door for forty-five minutes clutching her latte.

She wasn't surprised by his absence.

At the Book Shelf, she tried calling his condo several times. He didn't have an answering machine, so she listened to the ringing for several minutes, a hypnotic pulse she didn't want to sever. She considered calling Charles at his job, but she didn't have the number.

By noon, she had picked out four books from the mystery-thriller section to give him, gifts, and she planned to pen a card that would read: *To Charles, the next master of dark fiction.*

At the same time, she felt surges of doubt. Why should *she* apologize? Taking the blame was a reflex, a remnant of old Ellen.

He had said mean things to her. All her life she had quickly assumed the guilt, accepted the hurt and felt sorry for herself, beginning with the departure of her father.

Maybe this was just another episode of her continuing bad relationships with men. Maybe men in general were to blame.

———

Later that day, while helping an older woman find the travel section, Ellen walked past the bookstore's café and caught a glimpse of romantic bliss, which taunted her.

Why is it so easy for other people to find true love?

A young couple sat at one of the little tables, enjoying their bagels and java, holding hands.

How peachy keen.

The older woman found the books on Rome she was looking for and Ellen left the travel section. She glanced back at the happy couple for one more masochistic stab of melancholy.

Then she stopped in her tracks.

Something about the young man looked familiar.

He looked like Seymour Ravenwood minus a generous number of pounds. Could it be George's oafish son?

A time warp quickly sucked her in. Being reminded of George at this moment, on top of everything else, felt like a bad dream.

Then she felt waves of guilt and embarrassment. She remembered staying hidden in the shadows as George dragged his son out of the Amber Hotel and back to Decatur. It was her weakness that had given them away—a phone call to her mother, accompanied by the easy admission of where they were hiding.

Ellen knew she had two options. She could avoid Seymour, hiding in the back shelves, which was a typical Ellen Gordon thing to do.

Or she could walk up to him, introduce herself and apologize.

She took one step backward, then several steps forward.

"Seymour, hi," she said.

He stared at her for a long moment before the light bulb kicked in. "Ellen…?"

"Yes. I work here."

"Ellen Gordon," he said, standing. "Wow."

"I know. It's been a while," she said.

"All this time…you stayed."

"Yes. You brought me here and I haven't left."

Seymour turned to the pretty, narrow-faced blonde who remained seated. She appeared uninterested in—maybe even threatened by—the appearance of a girl from his past. He explained to the blonde, "I know Ellen from high school. My dad used to date her mom."

"And rape me," Ellen announced to both of them, drawing shocked reactions…in the theater of her mind.

She wasn't *that* bold.

"Hi," said the blonde in a flat tone. "I'm Nikki."

Seymour was more animated. "You look great," he told Ellen. His eyes took her in, top to bottom.

"So do you," she said, which was the truth. "You really..." She stopped and let him say it.

"I know. I lost a lot of weight. Sixty pounds. I cleaned up. No more, you know..." He didn't specify, but she figured he was referring to drugs.

"You still see, what was his name...Racer?"

"God, no," he laughed. Then he said, "Your mom wised up. She dumped my dad."

"Yes, I know."

"He's a psycho. He is just...the worst."

"Seymour, I'm sorry," Ellen said.

He looked at her, puzzled. "For what?"

"It's my fault."

"What is?"

"That your dad found you...after you brought me here. I got scared. I called my mother. I told her the name of the hotel..."

"I know," said Seymour. "My dad told me everything. It doesn't matter now. That was years ago."

With those few, simple words, Ellen felt as though a weight had been lifted off her shoulders.

"You're doing well?" he asked. His eyes kept checking her out, and she realized that she probably really did look a lot different than in high school...prettier, more confident. In fact, to a certain extent, she had changed as much as he had.

As the conversation flowed, Seymour's girlfriend started giving him irritated glances and he finally noticed.

"Well, if you ever need anything..." he told Ellen, pulling out a pen. "Let me give you my number." He wrote out his number on a napkin.

She took it and thanked him.

He returned to the table with his blonde girlfriend who continued to look annoyed.

Ellen thought, *If she's threatened, I must be attractive.*

She hadn't seen Seymour in a long time and barely knew him…but still felt bonded to him in a special way.

They had both endured George Ravenwood. For that they deserved medals.

She realized she had forgotten to mention that she still had his fifth-grade spelling certificate. Was it strange that she had held on to it all these years? Would it be awkward to even bring up?

She gave Seymour one last glance. His focus had fully returned to the pretty blonde. So Ellen's attention needed to move on as well.

Her mind returned to Charles and the romance in her own life, which was still a total shambles.

"Okay," said Peg later that afternoon, gesturing Ellen to join her in a back aisle of the bookstore, away from needy customers. "Come here. Let's talk."

"What?" said Ellen.

"You don't look good."

"Thanks."

"No, really. You don't have to tell me anything, but when I see you look all glumpy like this, I gotta ask what's the matter and see if I can help."

"Glumpy?"

"Glumpy. It's a word I made up. It's like a combination of glum and grumpy, with a dash of frumpy. I use it on my sister all the time."

"Well then, I guess you could say I'm glumpy."

"Anything I can do to help?"

"No."

"Is it boy trouble?"

Ellen didn't answer, which became an answer.

"I'm right," said Peg. "I can smell boy trouble a mile away."

"I'd rather not talk about it."

"Did you and Charles have a fight?"

Ellen sighed.

"What's wrong?"

"It's…complicated."

"It can't be that complicated."

Ellen almost laughed. "No. It's *definitely* complicated."

"You know, I could fix you up."

"No. I'm not on the rebound. I'm just..." Ellen searched for what she really wanted and then frankly expressed it.

"I want to talk to him," she declared.

"Then talk to him. Problem solved. Call him up. Don't wait for him to call you. The phone works two ways, you know."

"He's not at home."

"Call him at work."

"I don't know the number."

Peg touched her arm with a look of mock concern. "There's this service provided by the telephone company. It's called Information. The number is 4-1-1."

"Sounds vaguely familiar," said Ellen, returning the sarcasm.

"Want me to write that down for you? Three numbers, 4-1-1."

"I think I've got it."

"Go use the phone in the back. Terri won't care. She spends half the day on it yelling at her teenagers."

Ellen nodded. She peered down the aisle. Terri stood by the registers, talking to one of the regulars, a widow who consumed half a dozen books a week.

Peg said, "Don't worry. I won't listen. I'll stay here, tending to *your* customers. But you have to tell me how it goes after."

Ellen said, "I knew there was a catch."

"Talk dirty to him. If he's got a boring job, nothing gets a guy more excited than a woody under the desk."

Ellen stepped into the back room and lifted the phone receiver off its cradle. She dialed Directory Assistance and wrote down the number for Technor.

Ellen dialed the company. The woman who answered had a sweet voice, eager to help and very polite.

But she had no listing for a Charles Balun. When Ellen persisted, the woman connected her with someone in Human Resources who was more definitive.

"We do not have an employee named Charles Balun and our records indicate that we never did. Somebody gave you some bad information."

Chapter Nineteen

When the urge tore up his innards, bubbling up in his throat like a surge of bile, he knew it was a duty, a higher calling, and any attempt to resist would fall in defeat.

He bounced off the walls of his apartment, pacing in circles for hours until his legs ached and head throbbed. He squeezed himself into his favorite chair, created elaborate mind plays, rewound them to favorite moments, froze the frame, shouted out directions to the cast, clutched himself, pulled his hair and drew his own blood as he conjured life-and-death struggles.

But it was all minor league. The mind plays did not seal the urges in a tight little box and send them packing. They didn't provide the necessary relief.

He hated the urges and cherished them all the same.

Convincing himself to conquer his next victim took less time than before. After all, success had been at his side for those earlier romps into the city shadows. Young women had been buried, transitioned from above ground to below, from laughter to tears.

And no one had come knocking on his door.

He was charming and suave. No one had reason to suspect a thing.

He loved the duality. He loved having more than one life. More lives made him feel more…alive.

A little after ten o'clock, he thrust himself into the night, armed with the blade.

Tonight's strike took a little longer. The weather had warmed—more spring, less winter—meaning that increased numbers of people sprinkled the sidewalks and alleys. Finding his prey and accomplishing his task without potential witnesses would be harder.

Like in a video game, he had advanced to the next level. A little less easy, but that was the challenge he would meet. Beating tougher odds would just make it more rewarding.

He was not going to postpone the inevitable for a colder night. Now, *that* would be torture.

He walked the neighborhood for an hour, searching out targets. On a few occasions, he found a candidate and followed her, only to be disappointed that she never offered the right moment, the proper cover or isolation.

If these women only knew what one wrong turn would have cost them...

In particular, he followed a tall woman with long, straight brown hair, prominent nose and chin and western boots. He relished the thought of cutting her throat while yanking back the head, pulling on a fistful of hair like a lever to expose a stretch of soft, waiting flesh. But she wasn't headed home—she entered a noisy pub, and he was not about to wait around for anybody.

After giving up on Cowboy Boots, he followed two Asian women, then a staggering drunk chick muttering to herself—most promising— but the optimum moment never arrived. The women entered buildings or cars or met with other people and spoiled all his fun.

At one fifteen a.m., a dam broke and a stream of new hopefuls poured forth. A concert had ended at Dreadlocks, a small but packed reggae bar, and dozens of young people, soaked in sweat and alcohol, spilled onto the street and sidewalk.

While the music inside was African reggae, the clientele leaned heavily toward white suburban chicks looking for urban adventure. They had made the trek via carpool or El train.

Most of them had come into the city with friends...but some had come alone to meet friends.

As the crowd diffused from a big glob into smaller groupings moving from the epicenter, he found a possibility, someone saying goodbye to friends and then heading off solo, a very good sign indeed. She had shaggy, spiky hair—not flattering—and a nose stud, which looked like a stray booger. She looked young—barely drinking age, or perhaps equipped with a fake ID.

It didn't matter to him. If she was old enough to test the dangers of the big bad city, she was old enough to become its victim.

She should have been wearing a coat—kids these days!—but wore instead a college sweatshirt with a hood. University of the Damned. He wondered if she felt the crisp air running through her clothing, chilling her tummy, hardening her nipples.

He smiled as she left the main road to take a narrow side street. She was heading for the El station, apparently choosing the shortest distance between two points instead of a well-lit route with regular traffic.

Good choice, honey. Thank you for my gift. I think I love you.

As he got closer, he could see the floral embroidered pockets on her jeans. The pockets lifted and fell in a nice rhythm with each other, like a teeter-totter. Her ass was biggish, baby fat, junk food. The hip-hugger jeans exposed her lower back almost to the butt crack. *Refrigerator repairman pants,* he thought to himself, and he chuckled.

Out loud. *Shit!*

She turned. He had a split second to reach a decision—make his move or surrender the opportunity—was it dark enough, isolated enough? No time to think—

Act.

He moved toward her quickly, a straight line, fierce and direct, a thirty-foot dash, leaving no doubt of his intentions, and she let out a little gasp, the beginnings of a yelp, and he hated doing it this way, with the victim facing him, because sneaking up from behind was so much easier, allowing for a powerful first strike, and then he realized he didn't have the blade drawn yet and he wasn't wearing the ski mask, and God damn it, everything was wrong wrong wrong and now she was going to scream loud into the night and run away—

Instead, she crumpled.

She fell to the ground in a pile. He reached her and looked down.

A gift from the heavens?

He glanced around. He saw no one. He looked back at her.

She had fainted.

A terrified little suburban girl, light-headed with alcohol, her mind already alive with paranoid fears about the city before he even showed up.

His arrival was just the icing on the cake. A confirmation.

He looked at the surroundings. There were too many apartment buildings, back porches, windows, parked cars.

There was a gravel alley up ahead. The alley continued underneath the elevated train tracks. The tracks led to a platform perhaps two blocks away—no doubt, her destination.

He grabbed her by the tennis shoes—pink, practically lost inside her frayed bell-bottoms—and dragged her along the gravel, away from the street.

It made noise. Somewhere, a dog barked.

Damn dog.

Here he had a perfectly passive victim, someone to play with, and the environment was all wrong. He needed a garage, a shed, a basement, a laundry room, a—

Dumpster.

There was a large steel Dumpster, covered in illegible graffiti, against the side of an apartment building.

He dragged her quickly to the Dumpster, pebbles bouncing in her wake. She was chubby, but he was strong, and he shoved her up and over the lid of the Dumpster.

She landed softly in garbage.

He saw car headlights in the distance.

He jumped into the Dumpster with her.

He closed the lid over both of them. Everything disappeared into complete darkness and utter stink. He stuck his hands into the loose trash. He found the warmth of her bare back under her sweatshirt, amid the coldness of food wrappers, newspapers, bottles and cans.

"Honey," he told her, "You have just been thrown away."

The sound of a car engine filled his ears.

He heard the vehicle drive past them, through the alley, grinding through the gravel, louder and louder, and then fading away.

She stirred.

"Oh...oh..." she said, little gasps.

"Don't speak," he said.

"Where am I?"

Was she deaf? He shoved his hand in the direction of her voice, missed, struck garbage, and she let out a short shriek. She began thrashing.

The first stab of the knifepoint hit gold.

"Oh my God!" she cried out, a groan and a wail.

"Don't talk or I do it again."

She obeyed. Soft crying did not constitute talking, not technically.

He liked it in here, just the two of them, holed up and pressed together, interwoven, master and servant, rolling in refuse. His nostrils became inflamed from the stink, but it didn't bother him because he was pleased she was experiencing the same sensation.

"I'm bleeding..." she whimpered.

"What did I say about talking?"

She shut up, except for her breathing, which was labored.

"That's right," he said. "Stay quiet."

"Why..."

"Ssshhh!"

He waited in silence for his moment to arrive. The only sounds came from their bodies occasionally shifting, causing trash to tumble around them.

Suddenly a happy melody chirped near her, electronic tones singing a song.

He jumped, and she said, "My cell phone—"

"Give it to me."

He felt her hand moving between them, pressing past his groin, fumbling for the cell phone, which grew louder.

He snatched it from her. He flipped it open.

A little blue square illuminated them. He saw her face up close— mouth gaping, eyes enlarged, hair filthy with garbage.

He jabbed a button, connecting with the caller. He didn't say hello. He waited.

After several seconds of static, a woman's voice said, "Amy?"

"M-Mom," said Amy, and he moved the blade to her chin, making sure the phone light illuminated the short distance between life and death.

Amy shut up.

He spoke into the phone. "Amy can't come to the phone right now."

"Who is this?"

"A friend."

"Amy is supposed to come straight home after the concert."

"Amy says you're a horrible bitch of a mother. She says you beat her and raped her with a broom handle."

The woman gasped. *"Who is this?* Put my daughter on the phone."

At that precise moment, he heard a distant rumbling and knew that the time was near.

"Perfect," he said into the phone. "You get to listen."

"Put her on *right now!"*

"I'm going to place the phone against her mouth. I might even shove it down her throat so you can listen really good."

"I'm calling the police!"

The rumbling grew louder, as if a powerful force hurtled in their direction. The Dumpster started to vibrate.

"Steven!" shouted the woman on the phone. "Get on the line! A crazy man has Amy's phone!"

"Good! Get Steven on the line!" he shouted as the rumbling intensified, growing closer. "I want Steven to hear this too. It's a family affair!"

The rumbling became a rolling roar, booming above the Dumpster, and then he had the perfect moment he was waiting for. The El train moved directly over them like a monstrous dragon, shaking the Dumpster with a blanket of roars, and he slashed his prey with the blade, up and down and across, like a mad painter attacking a canvas, and she screamed—

She screamed very loudly, hopelessly lost in the noise of the train pulling into the station, her outburst creating a harmony with the screeching brakes.

As he sunk the blade into the countless possibilities on her body, he simultaneously smashed the phone against her teeth with his free hand, an orgy of sound for Mommy and Daddy.

Amy's scream had great character. Everybody has a different death scream, he thought, like fingerprints. Amy's outburst was hysterics, an extended cry, different than the goofy chokes of Oranjacket, or the sharp blasts of wailing from Parking Lot Girl.

He wished he could capture the delicious screams of his victims for posterity, playing them back again and again in the privacy of his home like listening to sweet music. He made a mental note to buy one of those handheld digital recorders and start archiving the Sound of Death. Begin a scream collection! He liked that.

Amy's screams continued strong through the cuts, like a balloon that would not puncture. When her scream wouldn't let up, he joined her. He screamed. He tried to top her scream. They created a lovely duet that continued as the train pulled out of the station. "*AAAAA! EEEE!*" Their voices tangled like exuberant lovers experiencing a joint orgasm.

As the cover of the train noise faded, the concerto needed to end. Surely, young Amy must be worn out? Yet he still heard screaming...

And then he realized it wasn't Amy.

The screams came from the cell phone, tinny and shrill.

He moved the blue square of light up and down and sideways to obtain piecemeal glimpses of his work, adding the images up in his head like a picture puzzle. The sum of his efforts was impressive. Most of the stabs had opened her up. Amy was limp, wet, dead. She couldn't make any more noise. In fact, during the frenzy of his attack, he had stuffed garbage in her wailing mouth—last night's lasagna, lettuce, kitty litter—whatever he could grab in fistfuls and shove down her bulging throat.

He brought the cell phone up to his face. The phone had cracked open a bit, hinge busted like an elbow bent the wrong way, but still working, as if in defiance.

"What is happening?" wailed Amy's mother.

"Glad you asked," he said. He heard her involuntary hiccups, remnants of a hard sobbing. "Your daughter has been thrown out in the trash."

"We're tracing this call," said Amy's father.

"You won't get here in time," he responded. "So you might as well shut up and listen to what I'm going to do next."

"Put Amy on the phone *now!*" said the father, and the mother chimed in with chants of "Amy! Amy! Amy!" that collapsed into more sobs.

He told them, "This is what it sounds like when someone's eyes are carved out of their head by a hunting knife. Listen carefully—you might be able to hear the blood squirt..."

But they wouldn't listen. They just screamed and hollered. He conducted his work anyway. Then he broke the cell phone into tiny bits of plastic and metal.

Before he made his exit from Amy's tomb, he had to wait for a rolling band of chatter to pass by—a group of kids making their way through the alley.

He shifted slightly, which caused noise, as some cans and debris spilled from one side of the Dumpster to another.

"Did you hear that?" said a young male voice.

"Probably a raccoon..." said another.

"Shit, let's get out of here. Those things are mean..."

Chapter Twenty

Ellen yawned until her eyes watered, tired from a long night of sporadic sleep, having spent too many hours tossing and turning in the dark replaying her last conversation with Charles. She wished she had said some things differently. She resented several of his more biting remarks. She wanted to go back in time and rewrite their dialogue, patch some holes, but the damage had been done.

She needed her steaming cup of caffeine this morning more than ever. Stepping into Pacific Coast Coffee, entering her old routine, she wasn't really looking for Charles anymore or expecting to see him.

But there he was.

At first she didn't recognize him. His hair was uncombed, tossed around and sticking up in bunches. He had not shaved, creating a screen of darkness over the bottom half of his face. His eyelids hung heavy. His entire body hunched over a tabletop.

He was writing in a notebook.

She stopped for a moment, uncertain of what to do. Should she go to the counter and place her order—pretending not to see him?

Or was this a chance to approach him and reconcile?

She hated confrontation. Every bone in her body urged her to stay away. Charles looked, well, glumpy. And gross, like he hadn't showered in a while.

The old Ellen would have turned around and slipped out the door, heading down the street to the convenience store for second-rate coffee, just to avoid a difficult encounter.

But she was determined not to be the old Ellen.

"Excuse me," said a man standing near her. "Are you in line?"

"No," she answered, and it determined her course of action.

"Hi, Charles."

She stood before him.

He glanced up. He immediately shut the notebook. It was a new one with a green cover, same style as the red one he had retrieved from her.

He didn't smile. He looked awful, as if he had slept less than she had.

"Hello, Ellen," he said.

She realized she hadn't rehearsed anything to say. She said the first thing that came to her mind.

"I'm sorry."

And he responded, "I'm sorry too, Ellen."

It sounded genuine, heartfelt. She experienced an immediate warmth spreading inside.

"Do you want to sit down?" he asked.

"Sure." She took the chair across from him.

For a moment, neither one of them spoke.

She gestured to the coffeehouse surroundings. "Old habits die hard."

"Very true," he said.

"I think there's something in the coffee here that's addictive," she said. "There ought to be an investigation."

Another moment of silence passed. Charles continued to lean on the green notebook, covering it with his arms. Lines of concentration formed on his forehead. "Ellen," he said. "I'm not happy with the way I acted toward you. It was wrong. You're one of the few good things to come into my life in a long time. I don't want to send you away. I know I can be an emotional roller coaster. I know I have a temper. I know you didn't mean any harm by taking the notebook."

"I should have left it alone when I found it, but the writing spoke to me," she said. "I kept waiting for the right time to tell you, but I was afraid. I knew it was messed up, reading someone's personal diary..."

"*Novel*," he corrected, and he chuckled dryly. "Let's not have that argument again."

"Right. Of course."

"You need to bear with me. I haven't been in a whole lot of meaningful relationships," he said. "I know that's not an excuse…"

"I'm in the same place," she told him. "This is new to me, too."

"A lot of what you read in that journal…while it's fiction, of course…it's also grounded in some degree of reality," said Charles. "The emotions of it. I had a really terrible childhood, Ellen. That's a fact."

"I did, too. That's why your words were so powerful to me. There was this connection that I've never felt before with anyone."

"But that's not what I want our relationship to be about."

"I know."

"I don't want to connect on that level. I'm trying to get away from the past, not embrace it. I'm purging it on paper—all the bad things, they've manifested into this character I've created, this fictional persona who becomes a killer. I'm extracting all of that and sending it on this course of destruction. I don't want you attracted to it, even on some sympathetic level. That's why the notebook was never meant for anyone to read. It's an exercise, an exorcism. If we are going to have a relationship, it's got to be based on the person you see here, in the flesh, in the present, and we have to leave the person in the notebook behind."

"I can do that," she said.

"It means we don't discuss the character in that notebook any longer."

She couldn't help staring down at the new notebook on the table, under his arms.

"You're still writing. Is it more of the same?"

"It's personal," he said. "For my eyes only. And I'm not going to lose this one."

"Fair enough."

"There are some things that are meant to remain private. We all have a part of ourselves that must not see the light of day. You can see me naked anytime…" He tapped the green notebook cover and smiled. "But not *this* naked."

She smiled, feeling a little jolt of arousal. It was the word *naked* that did it, coming from his lips.

She said, "Can we have a fresh start?"

"I'd like that."

"We'll go slow."

"I'd like that, too."

"Everything moved so fast these past few days, so intense... I think it became overwhelming."

"I agree."

"Maybe we can get together again on Friday."

"We'll have a low-key date. No crazy nightclubs, no fights with drunks."

"We can rent a movie and have dinner at my place," she suggested.

"I'd like that. Just the two of us."

As she stared at him, she wanted very badly to ask about his job at Technor. It remained a loose end. The woman at the switchboard had told her there was no listing for him. Maybe there was a simple answer, but she wanted to hear it from Charles. She thought about bringing the subject up and chose to save it for another day. They had made good progress here. She didn't want to jeopardize it with a new accusation. The question about his job could wait.

He gave her a hug before they parted. It was solid and real. She felt good inside again. The reconciliation felt right, like two puzzle pieces coming together, a perfect fit.

She told herself to never mention the red notebook to him again.

On her way to work, she thought about the molestation she had suffered in childhood. Maybe Charles was right. Certain things deserved to stay buried. It was twisted to leverage them for some kind of romantic bond.

But now there was something new that nagged at her, even though she fought hard to keep it out of her thoughts, where it could only cause trouble.

What was he writing in the green notebook?

Ellen arrived at the Book Shelf to find Terri's entire staff grouped together, buzzing in conversation.

Their faces looked stunned, serious. As Ellen stepped closer, she heard, "They say it's a serial killer, because there have been three murders, all in the same area, killed the same way."

"A serial killer?" Ellen asked, joining the circle.

Peg turned to her. "A girl from Wilmette was killed last night in an alley near Irving Park and Broadway."

"Oh, my God," said Ellen, feeling a surge of fear. "That's right near where I live."

"I know," said Peg. "Me too."

"My friend Jack is a detective with the police department," said Karen, a husky-voiced co-worker. "He knows the cops who were on the scene."

"Tell her about the eyes," said Peg.

"This hasn't been in the papers, but the killer takes out his victims' eyes."

Ellen gasped.

"I wonder if he does it before or after he's killed them," said Peg.

"Gross, gross, gross!" squealed Debbie, a chubby nineteen-year-old who worked in the bookstore cafe.

"Get this," said Karen. "Last night, when he killed the girl, he made her parents listen on a cell phone."

Ellen felt light-headed. Her vision frayed along the edges. "I don't think I want to hear this…"

"Are you going to pass out or barf?" Peg asked.

"I'm okay," said Ellen, turning away from her.

"I'm going to buy a taser gun," said Peg to the others. "No way that maniac is going to get me. I'll fry his ass."

Ellen felt her knees buckling and slumped against a table of new releases.

Bradford, the lone male co-worker, approached the group with quick footsteps, holding up a paperback. "This is the book I was telling you about."

Karen, Deb and Peg crowded around him. Ellen turned to look. It was a mass-market paperback with a lurid cover.

"*See No Evil*," said Bradford, "by Robert Walker. It came out last year. I'll show you…" He began searching through the pages. "In it, there's a killer who does the same thing. He pulls out the eyeballs of his victims, so they can't identify him in the afterlife."

"Maybe the killer is Robert Walker," said Peg.

"Maybe the killer is imitating this book," said Bradford.

"I have to show that book to Jack," said Karen. "Wouldn't that be incredible if we helped solve the case?"

"We'd be on TV, for sure," said Deb.

"Girls and guy," said Terri, approaching them, clapping her hands together. "The store is opening. Let's split up. And let's not talk about the murder in front of the customers, please. This needs to be an 'up' atmosphere for our guests. Don't forget your smiles."

Terri walked over to Ellen, who remained leaned against the table, head lowered. "Sweetheart, you okay?"

"Just a dizzy spell," said Ellen.

"I know. It really shocked me when I heard it, too. There are so many crazies out there. I hope you girls are careful. I feel so bad for that family, those poor parents…"

"Terri, you gotta see this," Bradford interrupted, waving a copy of *See No Evil*, split open to a specific page. "Read this part." Terri glanced down, read a few paragraphs and then jerked her head back, wrinkling her nose.

"Thanks, that's lovely, Bradford," she said.

"The killer in this book rips out the eyes of his victims, just like what happened to the girl in the Dumpster," Bradford said, excited, but Terri's response was bland.

"That's a book. This is reality," she said. "I'm sure there's no connection."

———

Ellen couldn't stop her mind from wandering throughout the day. She barely heard the customers, responding to their needs in automatic-pilot mode, speaking very little, but still managing to be efficient. The customers seemed far away, even when standing in front of her.

Ellen felt a new wave of the horrible suspicions she had tried desperately to suppress. She needed to rule out the possibility that Charles was the killer once and for all. Could she confront him about it? Would she be able to read the answer in his eyes? Had he offered any clues she had not recognized?

He had looked awful that morning, sloppy and drained.

She had seen that he was capable of brutal violence, when he attacked Jeremy. If she hadn't stopped him, would he have killed Jeremy?

She pictured the green journal in her mind. Something had driven him to fill pages in a new notebook. Something uncontrollable that he had to purge?

It all felt ludicrous. At the same time, she couldn't shake the possibility.

She wished the police would catch this killer fast and put her imagination to rest.

She thought about her conversation with Charles earlier that morning and how it had put her at ease after a long night of anxiety.

She wanted to find him and talk to him again, be reassured that he couldn't possibly be the killer of these girls.

One fact offered her solace: Charles lived outside the community of the three killings. He had told her that he lived near downtown in an upscale condominium high-rise on the Gold Coast on Chicago's Near North Side. Why would he commute to commit the murders?

Nothing made sense.

She decided to do something then that was totally out of character, yet could provide clues about the real Charles.

She planned to pay a surprise visit to him at his condo. He had never invited her over. If she could see him in his own environment, perhaps it would yield a clue. She would ask him about his day at work — and possibly learn whether or not he truly worked at Technor.

First, she needed an excuse for the drop-in visit.

Ellen used her employee discount to buy the brand-new thriller by James Patterson. She knew he liked Patterson and had talked about getting this book in particular.

After work, she drove toward the Gold Coast, remembering that he said he lived at the corner of Lincoln Avenue and LaSalle Street.

Fighting traffic all the way, she followed Lincoln Avenue until it ended at the park, just south of Lincoln Park Zoo. She did not see an intersection with LaSalle Street. She retraced her path—perhaps she had missed it? Finally she stopped at a gas station for directions.

The attendant looked at her as if she was crazy. "There's no such intersection," he told her. "The streets never meet. LaSalle hits a dead end several blocks from here."

Ellen hurried back to her car. She slammed the door and covered her face with her hands. She wanted to scream.

Was everything a lie?

Was his name even Charles? Or was it Darren?

Chapter Twenty-One

Peg Shore lived four blocks east of Ellen on the second floor of a handsome four-story Lakeview brownstone, occupying a two-bedroom unit that she had once shared with a sensitive and snippy roommate, Trish. After ongoing quarrels over everything from boys to dirty dishes, Trish moved out to live with a second cousin. Peg held onto the apartment, half-heartedly advertising for a new roommate while her well-to-do parents helped subsidize the rent, sending her monthly checks from one of Chicago's wealthiest lakefront suburbs. The extra space often accommodated men of various types: one-nighters, three-week trial boyfriends, seasonal flings, and even a six-month romance (exclusive for at least three of those six months).

Peg called her bookstore stint a "short-term, full-time job." She was always on the verge of advancing to something else, but without any real plans. She encouraged her parents by pursuing a college degree, even if it was in slow-motion, one night class per semester at a community college, successfully targeting Bs. "I'm in no hurry, as long as I graduate while they're still alive to see it," she had once told Ellen.

During their time together at the Book Shelf, Ellen had gotten to know Peg fairly well and even considered her a friend, although they didn't socialize much outside of the job. They were two very different personalities, but gravitated to each other, finding a complementary fit in each other's company.

Ellen felt like she was about to have an emotional breakdown over Charles, overwhelmed by his riddled back history and inconsistencies. She knew she needed to speak to someone, share everything, and get an outsider's view of this madness. Ellen's choice was Peg.

146 / Brian Pinkerton

"Come on over," said Peg on the phone, sounding more than eager to oblige. "Tell me everything that's going on, no detail is too personal. I'd be happy to help in any way that I can."

"This is just between the two of us," said Ellen, well aware of Peg's tendency to gossip.

"Absolutely," said Peg, adding, "What toppings do you want on your pizza?"

Ellen and Peg sat on the floor of Peg's living room, pizza box open between them, bottles of Heineken at their sides.

Before Ellen could even get the conversation started, Peg asked, "Have you slept with him?"

Ellen blushed and looked down at the carpet.

Peg squealed and said, "Way to go, girl."

"That's not what this is about."

"I know, sorry," said Peg. "Just had to get that out of the way."

"I'm worried," said Ellen, "that I don't really know him. That he hasn't been totally honest with me about some things. He's very guarded."

"Welcome to the world of men," said Peg, taking a long chug from her beer.

"It's more than that," said Ellen. "I've seen him…get violent."

"Toward you?" Peg straightened up.

"No, no," said Ellen. "He's been very gentle and caring toward me. It was a fight outside a bar. But that's not everything. He's also written…about some things. And now…with these murders happening in the neighborhood… I'm wondering…"

"No way!" said Peg, breaking out in a grin. "You think Charles is a serial killer?"

"I know," said Ellen. "It sounds ridiculous to even say this. But he's…different. And I feel he's covering something up. He's been lying to me about some things." Ellen sighed. "I guess I better start with the notebook."

"What notebook?"

Ellen said, "I'm going to tell you some things, but they are just between you and me. It can't go any further. If Charles knew…"

"You think I'm going to call him up and tell on you? Get real."

"I know. It's just…" Ellen sighed. "Complicated."

Ellen started at the beginning.

She told Peg about finding the notebook. She discussed her emotional connection with the troubled, lonely voice in the writing and the shared bond of childhood trauma. She talked about meeting Charles and dating him while secretly holding on to the notebook and continuing to read it.

She described the writing's increasingly dark tone and the emergence of Darren, the evil brother.

"Toward the end of the journal, Darren's voice takes over and he's talking about committing a murder," Ellen told Peg. "And it's in the same handwriting as the rest of the journal, like a split personality."

"Amazing," said Peg. "I have got to read that notebook. Can I borrow it?"

"He took it back," said Ellen. "He found the notebook in my apartment, and there was a big blowup. That's when everything fell apart. He couldn't believe I had it and never told him."

"What did he say about Darren and the murder?"

"He said it was all made up. It was part of a story he was writing."

"Then maybe it was."

"I don't know. It didn't read like fiction to me."

"Then it's well-written fiction."

"It read more like a diary."

"There are a lot of novels written that way."

"I'd believe him more if he hadn't lied to me about other things. Like his job and where he lives. There are so many plot holes in his own story that I can't determine what's real and what's fake."

Peg said, "I've seen Charles in the bookstore a bunch of times. He doesn't seem like the crazy type. He's quiet, but I can't see him killing women and cutting out their eyeballs…" She started to bite into a slice of pizza, then jerked her head back and nearly choked. "Wait a minute. *Wait a minute.*"

Ellen looked at her.

"I just remembered something," said Peg. She put down her pizza. "You know that book that Bradford was waving around today? *See No Evil* by Robert Walker?"

"The book where the killer cuts out the eyes?"

"This is freaking me out," said Peg, putting a hand over her mouth. "Holy shit."

"What is it?"

"I remember selling that book to Charles like six months ago."

Ellen felt her stomach turning over. "Oh no…"

Peg waved a hand. "Now let's not get carried away. I sold a lot of copies of that book. My grandmother read it. Still…"

Ellen said, "Peg, what should I do?"

"I don't know. This is freaky. But we don't have enough evidence to conclude anything. We need to do some more investigating."

"Like what?"

"Well, for starters, we need to get that notebook back."

"No way. He'll never let it out of his sight again. Besides, he's started writing a new one."

"A new one?" Peg looked at Ellen. "How do you know?"

"I saw him writing in it this morning at Pacific Coast Coffee."

"Would he let you read it?"

"God, no."

"Your answers may lie in what he's writing about now."

"I thought about that, too."

"What if we stole it—I mean, *borrowed* it? If it matches up with what's happening…the other murders…then we'll know for sure. We can go to Karen's friend Jack, the police detective."

"I don't see how this is going to work."

"What do these notebooks look like?"

"What do you mean?" asked Ellen.

"The covers, the brand."

Ellen thought back to the red notebook. It was a standard, spiral-bound, three-hole-punch, student notebook.

"The cover on the red one said something like 'class' or 'classroom'."

"Is the green notebook the same?"

Ellen searched her memory and nodded. "Yes. I'm pretty sure it is."

"Easy," said Peg. "We go to the store and we find an identical notebook. Then you and I go to Pacific Coast Coffee. You talk to Charles, create a diversion. I swap notebooks without him seeing. We take the one he's writing in. We get out of there, go someplace and read it. If it talks about more killings and they match up to the Lakeview murders, we go to Jack the Detective. We could help solve the case and become famous. I bet we'd get on TV."

"No, no," said Ellen. Her mind was swimming. "I don't like this."

"Why not? I'm kind of digging it."

"What if he's just writing more fiction? If we take his notebook…If I do it a second time, that's the end of the relationship right there."

"So what?" said Peg. "There are more fish in the sea."

Ellen shook her head. "No. It's not that easy." She had spent her entire life looking for a romance this heartfelt.

Peg could read the reaction on Ellen's face.

"Listen," said Peg. "I know how you feel. You might even think you love this guy. Maybe you haven't had a lot of relationships so you don't want to let go of this one, but let me tell you something from the voice of experience, too much experience some would say—all men are interchangeable. Sure, their bodies may look a little different, their hobbies might vary, their sense of humor might be better or worse, but in the end, they're just men, with a limited range of emotions, good for a few things, like sex, companionship, fixing stuff, paying the check at dinner." Peg started laughing at her own analysis.

Ellen wasn't laughing. "I feel different about Charles."

"Sure you do," said Peg with a dismissive tone. "Listen, I have a lot of guy friends. I'll fix you up with someone. You won't even have time to rebound. In fact, there's this guy, Pete, he's cute and I think you would really hit it off. Pete Brent. He's an architect."

"Thanks," said Ellen, "but I don't think so."

"Come on," said Peg. "Charles has lied to you about things, he's writing freaky shit in notebooks. Even if he's not the killer, why do you want to hang out with him? I know, he's really good looking, but take it from me, the excitement from that wears off after six weeks, and then you have to deal with their *brains*…"

"I'm not ready to split up with him," said Ellen. "Not now."

"But you're the one worried he's a maniac killer."

"You said yourself that it's far-fetched," said Ellen sharply. "You just like the idea of playing Nancy Drew and stealing his notebook to see what's in it."

Peg frowned. "I think maybe you get off on thinking he might be dangerous. It's like those women who send marriage proposals to serial killers in jail. I heard that Drew Peterson receives…"

"Stop it," said Ellen. Her tone had an unusual forcefulness to it.

Peg went silent and drew a deep breath. "Okay," she said. "Whatever. Do you want another beer?"

Ellen said, "Yes."

As Peg got up to head for the kitchen, she turned to Ellen and said, "Let me just say one more thing and then I'll drop it. Once they start lying to you about the little stuff, like their jobs or what their parents do, then the big stuff usually isn't far behind—like cheating on you and seeing other women."

Peg's voice turned uneven, and Ellen knew she was speaking from personal experience, old wounds that had not healed.

Ellen looked down at the crumbs in the pizza box and wished she had not come over and started this entire conversation.

It was shortly after nine p.m. when Ellen returned to her apartment. As she stepped through the door, she heard the telephone ringing.

She sprinted across the room and grabbed it. "Hello?" she said, out of breath.

"Hello," said a deep, gravelly voice. "And how are you this fine evening?"

Ellen didn't recognize the caller. "Fine. Who is this?"

The voice responded, "This is Darren."

Ellen's blood ran cold. Her heart raced. She didn't know what to say or do. "Darren?"

"I've wanted to meet you for a very long time, Ellen."

She almost dropped the receiver but hung on. She couldn't think of a response. Her breathing turned choppy. Her lips trembled and her feet wanted to run...but where?

Then the person on the other end laughed.

His tone lightened and became familiar. "It's me, Charles. I'm just kidding with you." After a long silence, he said, "Hello?"

"Oh," said Ellen, heart still pounding. "You...startled me."

"I'm sorry," said Charles. "I thought it would be funny, given all the, you know. I didn't mean to frighten you. I'm just goofing around."

"Real funny," said Ellen, unamused.

Charles said, "You didn't really think...?"

"No," said Ellen. "Of course not."

"Good. Then you know how ridiculous this whole thing is?"

"Ridiculous. Yes." Ellen's head was spinning.

"I'm looking forward to our date night tomorrow," said Charles. "I just wanted to see if I could bring anything. How about a bottle of wine? You pick the movie, I'll pick the wine."

"Sure. That would be fine," said Ellen.

"And Darren will bring the dessert."

"*Charles*, stop it," said Ellen sharply. "It's not funny."

"All right, all right," said Charles. "I'm not trying to upset you. I just wish you wouldn't take everything so seriously."

"I take *you* seriously," said Ellen. "That's why I don't like this joking around about...Darren."

"Okay," said Charles. "I'm sorry. I'll leave him at home. I promise."

Chapter Twenty-Two

Peg Shore typically woke up at the last possible minute, dressed quickly, ignored breakfast, grabbed the bus moments before it pulled from the curb and made it to the Book Shelf with one minute to spare. She enjoyed her night life, which made her a lousy morning person. At work, she applied her makeup in the ladies' room and then jump-started the day with a cup of coffee from the bookstore's café.

On this particular morning, however, she stepped out of her routine. Her digital alarm clock triggered earlier than usual, displaying a readout she rarely witnessed. Waking up extra early sent an ache throughout her bones. Fortunately, her brain kicked into high alert. She had a mission.

Ellen would not go along with Peg's scheme to obtain Charles's new journal, so Peg chose to go it alone. She was going to nab that green notebook. Ellen would thank her later. The girl was simply too timid to make such a bold move. Fortunately, Peg had plenty of courage and liked a good challenge.

First, Peg had to find an identical notebook for the swap.

Ellen had described the notebook as spiral-bound, three-hole punch, and branded "class-something" on the cover.

Peg's search began at Walgreens. She entered the school supplies aisle and found a shelf with several stacks of notebooks.

But nothing with the word "class" on the cover.

No problemo. She advanced to the next drug store on her list, Hooper's, a few blocks away. She dug through another series of notebook stacks, and then found one staring her in the face that was labeled *First Class Notebook 10 ½ in. x 8 in./wide rule/270 sheets.*

She continued flipping through the pile, excited. The First Class line of notebooks offered a rainbow of colors: yellow, red, blue, black, orange...and green.

She bought the green one.

Outside the store, she roughed up her purchase to remove the appearance of newness. It needed to look worn.

Then Peg placed the notebook in her handbag and headed for Pacific Coast Coffee.

Peg had been inside the establishment once or twice before with boyfriends who led her there "the morning after". She didn't remember it much. For her, all these coffeehouses felt the same. Plus, they were stupidly expensive. Unless a boy was treating, she didn't need to fork over a big wad of cash for a cup of caffeine.

Pacific Coast Coffee bustled with business. There were three lines at the counter and most of the tables were occupied.

Peg glanced around, looking for Charles.

She almost missed him, because he looked so grubby. His head was down.

He had one of those faces that was quick to sprout whiskers. He wore an old gray sweatshirt, torn at one of the shoulder seams. And, sure enough, he was writing in a notebook with a black pen. His arm circled the notebook like a protective fence.

Peg thought about Ellen's descriptions of the content of Charles's writing: the dark and moody expressions, the split voices, the allusions to committing murder.

Right now, messy and hunched over with intensity in his eyes, Charles looked more than a little cracked.

A tall cup of coffee rested near his arm. Perfect.

Peg advanced.

"Charles. How's it going?"

He looked up as if being pulled from a nap. It took a moment for him to emerge from his fog and concentrate on her.

"Oh. Hi."

"How's the coffee today?"

Charles shrugged. "The same."

Peg stepped closer and Charles shut the notebook.

She observed that the cover was identical to the notebook she had purchased. It gave her a rush. At that moment, she knew she would succeed with her mad scheme.

"What are you working on?" she asked.

"Just writing."

"Do you come here often? I usually buy my coffee at the bookstore. Is the coffee here any good?"

Charles sighed, a signal that he was in no mood for conversation. "I suppose."

"I can't believe how many different types of coffee there are. Cappuccino, Frappuccino, mocha...so many choices, how do you choose? Well, I guess I'll go pick something. Today's my lucky day. I have a coupon in my purse..."

Peg grabbed her purse and swung it upward, striking Charles's cup of coffee. The coffee toppled off the table and into his lap.

"Jesus!" Charles leapt up from his chair, the crotch of his jeans soaked.

"I am so sorry!" gasped Peg. "Oh my God, I am such a klutz."

Charles attempted to wipe the mess with a napkin.

"Oh no, I'm really sorry," said Peg. "Did it get all over you?'

"I'm going to need more napkins," grumbled Charles. He headed for the counter, bow-legged and still dripping.

Peg had less than one minute to conduct the switcheroo.

She reached into her handbag and took out the new green notebook. She exchanged it with the one on the table and slipped Charles's notebook into her handbag.

When Charles returned, nothing looked out of place. He had fistfuls of paper towels. He continued wiping his pants and the chair. An employee came over with a mop and began working on the floor.

Peg offered Charles a five-dollar bill.

"Here—please—take it—buy yourself another cup of coffee. I feel terrible. I hope I didn't burn you."

"No," muttered Charles. "I'm okay."

"I guess I better go before I cause any more damage," said Peg. "Next time you come into the Book Shelf—free cup of coffee. My treat."

Charles didn't respond. He didn't accept her five-dollar bill, either. He was still wiping his pants, fighting to control his anger.

"Okay, bye," said Peg. "You can send me the bill." She gave one last glance at the notebook she was leaving behind.

Then Peg's heart seized up for a moment.

She saw an orange price tag on the cover—she had forgotten to remove it. It stood out like a bright blemish, an obvious difference from the notebook she had just nabbed from him.

She turned to Charles. He was looking at her. Then his gaze left her face to see what she had been staring at...landing on the notebook cover.

Peg turned and left.

She didn't look back. She nearly knocked into a woman with a tray full of coffees. She pushed open the front door and hurried out of the café to the sidewalk.

Peg walked swiftly, then advanced into a slow jog. She thought to herself, *Boy, that was close...*

Bang! Peg turned to see Charles emerging from the coffeehouse, slamming through the door, his face twisted with rage.

Peg ran.

Oh my God, he's going to kill me!

She ran through the crowd, zigzagging through openings between clumps of pedestrians, firmly clutching the handbag that contained the green notebook. She had to lose him.

Up ahead, several people waited at the curb for the light to change. A steady flow of traffic chugged past them.

Peg made a sharp left turn and headed down another street. She wished she had her running shoes on. Her thick heels slowed her down and she feared that he was gaining on her.

A fear that was confirmed when she heard his footsteps hitting the pavement behind her—getting louder and closer.

He wouldn't dare kill me in front of all these people?

Charles grabbed Peg by the wrist and she let out a short yelp, jerked toward him like a dog on a leash.

In a series of swift movements, he took the handbag, dug inside and retrieved the notebook.

Then he stared at her, hard, eyes blazing.

"What the hell is wrong with you?" he said through clenched teeth.

For a response, Peg could only offer, "I...I..."

Charles continued to look her over for a moment. Then he grunted in disgust, spun around and left. He headed back the way he had come. In seconds, he disappeared into the busy sidewalk crowd.

Peg rubbed her wrist where he had grabbed her. It was red. Her arm ached from being yanked.

She faced the direction where he had been, no longer seeing him, but still feeling his presence all around her, the fierce eyes, the tight grip.

Fear penetrated her skin, but she refused to let him get the best of her.

"Screw you, Charles," she said quietly. "This is only the beginning."

Chapter Twenty-Three

Ellen was stocking the magazine racks to start her morning at the Book Shelf when Peg walked over and said, "Hey, girl, what's going on?"

"Not much," said Ellen. "What's going on with you?"

"Oh…nothing," said Peg. "Same old same old."

Peg remained standing there, as if she had something more to say but didn't know how to say it. Ellen finished refreshing a row of home and gardening publications, then turned to Peg and said, "What?"

"I've been thinking about our conversation last night," said Peg.

Ellen looked at her warily. "You're not going to try to talk me into that notebook-swapping scheme again, are you?"

"No," said Peg, rubbing her wrist.

"Good."

"But, listen, I do think you need to take a deeper look at your situation." Peg stepped closer, lowering her voice. "The more I think about it—I don't think you should continue dating Charles."

"Why?"

"Well, because of all the things you told me."

"But I don't know for sure if he's connected to those killings. What if I'm wrong? It's a pretty big assumption. You know I have a crazy imagination. I read too many books."

"Then let's forget the murders for a minute. Apart from that, you have to admit, he's just plain weird. He's damaged goods. Didn't you say he had a messed-up childhood?"

Ellen bristled, feeling a rush of defensiveness. "You can't blame someone for having a messed-up childhood. You can't just write them off because of something they couldn't control, what people did to them. So he has psychological scars. That doesn't mean he's ruined and should be thrown out like garbage."

"Whoa," said Peg, hands raised, palms out. "Sorry. I didn't know this was a sore spot."

Ellen said, "I don't want to make any rash decisions. More than anything, I feel…confused. I have all of these feelings for him, but I'm also just not sure about so many things."

"Do you want some honest advice?" said Peg.

Ellen sighed. "I suppose."

"You're a good-looking young woman. You don't have an ounce of fat on you and I hate you for it. When you pay attention to your hair, dress up in good clothes, maybe highlight your eyes a little bit, you become a real catch. But here's the problem. I've known you for a while. I see how you interact with the customers and other people. You're shy. You have no confidence. No initiative. You walk around staring at the carpet. You look like you'll jump out of your skin if anybody touches you."

Ellen said, "Gee, thanks."

"Hey, honest advice," said Peg. "I'm just saying…there's no reason you can't go out and meet a lot of guys. You're your own barrier. You need to break through and experience more…how should I say this…you can't just fall in love with your first boyfriend. You have no reference points. Of course he's going to be the greatest, the one and only. But I think you can do better for yourself. You should move on."

"I don't spend all day looking at the carpet," said Ellen.

Peg rolled her eyes. "That's not the point."

"No. I know. It's true. I'm not running around with a new boyfriend every week like *some people*." She stared at Peg.

"Touché," said Peg. "I'm not the perfect role model. But maybe there's something in between slut and wallflower."

Ellen started to say something, then broke out laughing. "Boy, you just tell it like it is, don't you?"

"Look at that nice smile when you laugh," said Peg. "Christ, I hardly ever see it. Your whole face changes."

"The slut and the wallflower," said Ellen. "I think that would be a great title for a book."

"Do you see my point?"

"Sort of. You're saying I'm defending Charles because I'm desperate."

"No. Let's review the situation. Charles writes all this crazy shit in a notebook. Right?"

"Well, yes. But no crazier than half the books we sell."

"And you said he gets violent. That's not a good sign."

"He punched out somebody who was harassing me in a bar. He was just sticking up for me."

"Sure. And the next time he loses his temper, maybe it's your face he's punching in."

"I can't imagine that."

"Why are you protecting him? Is it because he's good-looking with a good bod? Because I can get you good-looking with a good bod."

"It takes more than that to turn me on."

"Okay. What if I throw in a good sense of humor and a lot of money?"

"What are you talking about?"

"His name is Pete Brent. I told you about him last night."

"Ah. So that's what this is all about. You want to fix me up."

"I've told him about you."

"And he didn't run off screaming?"

"He's been in the store. He's seen you. He says you're really cute."

"Really?" Ellen couldn't help feeling intrigued. "What day was it? What was I wearing?"

"It doesn't matter. He window-shopped and he liked what he saw. I told him you were into books, kind of quiet, and he's cool with that."

"You make it sound like reading books and being quiet is some sort of disease."

"No. The point is, he doesn't care if you're not outgoing. He's sort of quiet too, sometimes."

"What does he do?"

"He's an architect. It's a small company, but he makes really good money."

"How do you know so much about him?"

"He's a friend of a friend."

Ellen thought about it. She still had a date scheduled that night with Charles—Chinese food and a movie at her place. Just the thought of sharing the couch with Charles gave her a rash of goose bumps—the good kind.

"I'm not interested," she told Peg.

Peg displayed her disappointment openly. "Really?"

"Give me some more time to see where things are going with Charles."

"Well," said Peg. "Here's the thing. Pete and Kevin—the guy I'm dating—are dropping by the store today at two."

Ellen tensed up. "Then I won't be here. I don't like being pressured."

"You have to be here. It's your job to be here. If he needs help finding a book, you're going to help him."

"You are so pushy."

"You need a push."

"I think *you* need a push," said Ellen firmly.

Peg looked at her, surprised. "Are you suggesting getting physical? Maybe I was wrong about you. You don't need anybody to bring you out of your shell. You're already getting more aggressive."

"I'm sorry," said Ellen, trying to contain her anger.

"Don't be sorry," said Peg. "I kind of liked it. You should have seen yourself—you even stood up straight with backbone. That's what I've been talking about."

Ellen turned back to the magazine racks. "I have to finish with these magazines or Terri's going to be on my case."

———

Sometime shortly after two p.m., Ellen heard Peg greeting friends at the bookstore's front entrance. She tried to make a quick dash for the back room but in doing so stepped into view, a critical mistake.

"Hey, there's Ellen. Come here and meet Kevin and Pete!" called out Peg.

Ellen stopped in her tracks and said "Damn it" under her breath. She turned and flipped on the smile that Peg had liked so much. She walked over.

"Hi," she said. Peg stood with two young men, both good looking in a clean-cut, frat-boy kind of way. Which one was Pete?

Peg introduced them to her. Pete was tall and tan with blond hair and longish sideburns. He wore a ski jacket with a chair lift tag dangling from the zipper.

"Pete just got back from Aspen," said Peg. "That's why he's tan in Chicago in March."

"It'll be gone in a week and I'll be pasty again," Pete said.

Ellen felt self-conscious, knowing that Pete had seen her previously and allegedly called her "cute".

I wonder if I look cute today? Why did I wear these crappy old slacks and shoes?

Pete talked about the vacation he had taken with his brother. Kevin talked about a ski trip he had taken to Wisconsin, laughing as he described wiping out after too many beers. Ellen didn't ski, so she had nothing to contribute to the conversation. She listened and smiled and nodded.

"Are we still on tonight?" Peg asked them.

"You bet," said Kevin.

Peg turned to Ellen. "We're going to O'Dell's for drinks. You should join us."

"Yeah," said Pete. "Join us."

His personal invite startled her. He seemed nice enough, and he was handsome. But she wasn't about to break her date with Charles.

"Thanks," said Ellen, "but I can't. Maybe some other time."

Peg shot her a look that read, *You're blowing it, fool.*

"Okay, some other time," said Pete.

"I want to get trashed," said Kevin. "Next week I gotta start studying for my actuarial exam."

After Kevin and Pete left, Ellen tried to slip away. She combed the store looking for a customer to assist, but Peg caught up with her first.

"He practically asked you out!" Peg exclaimed.

"He said 'join us'."

"You know what he meant."

Ellen considered telling Peg that she already had a date planned with Charles, but decided not to go there. She didn't want to open up another discussion about Charles.

"At least tell me you'll consider joining us."

"I'll consider joining you," said Ellen, repeating Peg's words in a flat tone.

"Gee, you're welcome."

"Chitchat, chitchat," said Terri, approaching them, clapping her hands. "Break it up. This isn't the social hour. Peg, your friends have left, so let's get back to work."

Peg and Ellen parted, scooting in separate directions.

Ellen avoided Peg for the rest of the day, but every now and then Peg popped into view to blurt comments like, "Pete's family has a summer home on Lake Geneva," and "You'll change your mind..."

Chapter Twenty-Four

E llen worked on ambience.

She busied her mind with creating a clean, warm and inviting environment in her humble garden unit apartment. She fretted over the right music to play on the stereo and the appropriate volume, the best lighting level — dim but not dark — and even the position of the pillows on the sofa. She straightened the books in her enormous bookcase, which almost covered an entire wall. This was her beloved gateway to escapism. She wondered how many books she owned by now. Thousands? She cleaned the shelves of extraneous clutter and straightened the spines.

Charles would soon arrive for a date, featuring Chinese food and a movie rental, which left plenty of room for other things. The more she thought about Pete, Peg's well-intended but misguided effort to introduce her to a shallower, simpler man, the more Ellen felt her heart gravitate back toward Charles.

Charles had a magnetic presence, dark certainly, but accompanied by a hungry and powerful passion that could only grow out of heightened sensitivity and a wounded past. The two of them experienced a charged connection that few couples could match.

Tonight she would rid herself of any suspicions that Charles was connected to the recent killings. When she really cleared her head and thought hard about it, the notion was ludicrous. Still, she couldn't settle down until all doubt had been erased from her mind. After some wine and closeness, she would delicately ask him about some of the inconsistencies in the things he had told her.

She would tell him about trying to reach him at Technor. She would mention the attempt to visit his condo. Maybe she would even remark about the similarities between the recent murders and the book *See No Evil*, just to observe his reaction.

The old Ellen would not have been brave enough to bring those things up. But she would push them out, study the response, and conduct her own analysis. She didn't need Peg or Detective Jack or anyone else.

She was strong enough to stand on her own two feet.

The knocking on her door caused her to spring up from the couch, seized by an almost breathless excitement.

She hurried to let Charles in.

As he stepped into her apartment, she spontaneously kissed him. His face was clean-shaven, his hair neatly combed. He wore a bright sweater.

But his response to the kiss was flat. He didn't even smile.

Ellen said, "I can open the wine now, or we can go get a movie first."

Charles closed the door behind him. He looked down.

"What?" she said. "Charles, what is it?"

"We need to talk."

"What's wrong?"

He advanced into the living room, then paced in a semicircle before coming to a stop.

She walked over to him. "Charles? Are you okay?"

He looked up at her. His eyes fixed on her, hard and serious. "What was this little scheme you cooked up with your friend this morning?"

"Scheme?" she said. "What are you talking about?"

He studied her, as if examining her response for authenticity. The vagueness of his accusation filled her with anxiety. She said, "Charles, tell me, what is it?"

"Your little co-worker friend, the one with the freckles."

"Peg?"

"Yes."

"What did Peg do?"

"You don't know?"

"No, I don't. I swear."

"It doesn't make sense that she would act on her own. How would she even know?"

"Know what?"

"She tried to take my notebook this morning at Pacific Coast Coffee. She spilled coffee in my lap and then when I was distracted, getting cleaned up, she took my notebook. She tried exchanging it for a blank one so I wouldn't notice until she was gone."

Ellen brought her hands up to her face. "Oh, my God."

Charles took a step toward Ellen. "What did you tell her?"

Ellen felt a trembling ripple across her body. "I just—"

"What did you tell her?"

"Okay, okay," said Ellen, on the verge of tears, fighting them back. "I told her about the notebook. I know I shouldn't have. But these murders are happening in our neighborhood, and I was afraid. I told her about your notebooks, and that there was a new one. She wanted me to take your notebook so we could read it, and I said no. She must have done it on her own. I'm not a part of this. Does she still have it? I'll make her return it."

"I got it back. I had to chase her down the street. It was ridiculous."

"Charles," said Ellen. "I am so sorry."

"What did you tell her? Whatever you told her must have been pretty strong for her to want to steal my writing."

"You have to admit…" she said.

"Admit what?"

"There are coincidences."

"What coincidences? What are you talking about?"

"The murders!" Ellen raised her voice. "You wrote about committing murder while there are people being killed in this neighborhood."

He threw his hands in the air. "We've already talked about this. It's not real. Can't you tell the difference between fact and fiction? Jesus, Ellen, you work in a bookstore!"

"But why are these killings happening now?"

"I don't know! A full moon? This is crazy. You don't trust me. How can we have a relationship without trust?"

Ellen swallowed hard and said, "It's hard to trust you when you've been lying to me."

He looked her over. "I've been lying to you? About what?"

"Your job. Where you live. I tried calling you at work—"

"*Stop*," he said. He held up a hand. He started pacing again, looking at the floor, avoiding eye contact. Finally he sat down on the couch.

She remained standing in the middle of the room, watching him.

"I have not been totally honest with you about certain things," he said, speaking slowly. "I only did it...because I really like you. I was afraid that if I told you the truth on our first date, there wouldn't be a second date. I was going to come clean about it, but then all this crazy stuff about the notebook got in the way. Ellen, I don't have a manager position at Technor. I don't have a fancy condo on the Gold Coast. I'm unemployed."

He looked up at her.

"I want to be a writer," he said. "But I can't sell anything. I've been looking for work. My last job was custodian at an office building. My apartment is a few blocks away from here, basically one room, above a dry cleaners. It has cockroaches, an old sofa bed, a radiator that barely works and windows that leak. I'm still putting my life together and I didn't want you to see how incomplete everything is right now. It's not going to stay this way. I'm going to take night classes in the spring. I have plans. But I'm not a prize. I'm sure you could do better."

She walked over to him.

"No," she said. "You don't understand me then. I don't care about those things."

"Then you're a first."

"I'm a bookstore clerk living in a basement. Look around you. What's the difference?"

"Believe me, this is a palace compared with what I've got."

She sat next to him on the couch. She placed her arm around him. He continued to stare forward.

"They're going to be opening a new Book Shelf store downtown in the Loop," Ellen said. "They're already filling positions. I could talk to my boss, Terri, and get more information, a contact. You could work there. They're looking for people. You'd be surrounded by books all day long."

He turned and looked at her. "How's the employee discount?"

She smiled. "Twenty percent."

He leaned in and kissed her. She tightened her hold around him. He brought his hand up into her hair. She shut her eyes and moved her mouth along his lips, losing herself in the rush of adrenalin.

The phone rang.

"I'mnotgoingtoanswerit," she said, muffled in the kissing.

The ringing continued until the answering machine picked up. After Ellen's greeting, there was a beep and then Peg's voiced filled the room. She shouted to be heard over a din of dance music and voices.

"Ellen! It's Peg! We're at O'Dell's. Where are you? Pete is here! Say hi to Pete!"

"Hi, Ellen!" shouted Pete.

They sounded drunk.

"You were going to come join us! Get over here now!" Peg giggled. "Pete wants to hang with you! Hurry before his tan wears off!"

"Ellen, there's a beer waiting with your name on it!" said Pete.

"He likes your butt!"

"Don't tell her that!"

"Come find us! We'll be here! Try to get here by nine! Hurry! Bye!"

"Bye, Ellen!" said Pete.

"Bye, Ellen," said another male voice, probably Kevin.

At the click, Charles stood up.

"Wait," said Ellen.

"Obviously you've got somewhere else to go," said Charles.

"I already told her I wasn't coming."

Charles headed to the door. "This day isn't getting any better. I'd really like to leave."

"Please don't." Ellen followed, tears in her eyes.

Charles opened the door, then turned to face her.

"I can't be with you right now," he said. His voice cracked. "I'm sorry."

"Charles…"

"This just isn't going to work out," he said with finality.

Charles left, and Ellen faced a shut door.

Ellen wanted to smash the answering machine. She wanted to smash Peg.

Her apartment felt cold and empty, drained of the energy and promise of the last few hours.

She looked at the pillows on the sofa. She could hear soft strains of the light jazz she had chosen. It played easy and romantic, a cruel counterpoint to the paralyzing misery she felt inside.

Chapter Twenty-Five

He followed his prey.

She was drunk, an excellent bonus. Her footsteps landed in asymmetrical patterns, like a toddler, weaving to one side then the other as she moved down the sidewalk.

It was dark and late, another item on the checklist. He could follow her while staying in the shadows. Nobody watched him watch her. Most reasonable people were home asleep.

And most importantly, she was alone.

In the beginning, she had had young men on either side of her, also drunk, and they had talked in loud voices that bounced off the pavement. They had emerged from a Lakeview drinking hole, sensibilities watered down, showcasing their sloppy behavior and vulgarity. When they reached the corner of Ashland and Addison, the threesome stopped for more inane chatter, then said their goodbyes with lopsided bear hugs. They staggered off in three directions.

There would be action tonight.

He followed the girl with the happy, round, freckled face. She wore a pink coat and striped leggings. She hummed something to herself as she headed down a silent street of apartment buildings. She was surrounded by windows, a few of the squares lit up, but most of them dark and blank.

She headed up the walk of a brownstone, then did something that surprised him, and he almost got caught.

She stopped halfway and turned, looking away from her destination and into the night.

He ducked behind a parked car.

What the hell? He hadn't even put on his ski mask yet.

He cautiously peeked through the dirty windows of the car and saw her still standing there, looking around.

Was she suspicious? Could she sense his presence? Had he made a noise?

Then he saw someone approaching her from the other side of the street. It looked like a young man. In fact, it looked like one of the men she had just left.

"Pete," she said.

"Hey, Peg." The young man, blond-haired and wearing a ski jacket, walked up to her. They joined in a kiss.

"Kevin went home?" she asked.

"Yeah. I think he was disappointed that you didn't ask him to stay the night."

"Things change."

"Yes, they do." He kissed her again, this time for an extended period. Their jaws moved up and down as if they were chewing on one another. Then his hand went inside her coat for a little grope action until she shoved him away, giggling.

"Aw, come on," he said. "No one's watching."

"I'm out of beer. The fridge is on empty. We need more beer."

"Shit, really?"

"Can you go to the convenient mart? It's called Sandy's. It's like a block and a half away."

"I know where Sandy's is."

"You get the beer. I want Sam Adams in bottles. Then when you return, we'll have our own little party." She felt the crotch of his pants. "And you can bring Little Petie."

"This is so bad. If Kevin knew…"

"Screw Kevin. You saw how he was ignoring me tonight. So what? I have a better time with you. We'll tell him one day." Her voice was slurring all over the place. "Hurry up. If you take too long, maybe I will call Kevin."

"You're such a bad girl."

"That's for me to know and you to find out."

Pete headed back down the sidewalk, returning the direction from which he had come.

Peg entered the foyer, illuminated for a moment in white light. She took a key chain out of her purse, unlocked the inner door, and stepped inside. The door closed behind her with a loud thud.

From behind the parked car he watched her enter the building. He turned to look at Pete. Pete was near the end of the block. Then Pete turned and disappeared from view, probably not due to return for several more minutes.

He could still do this.

He had his knife and he had his brand-new handheld digital voice recorder. He was excited to begin his scream collection.

He remained crouched alongside the car. He stared up at her building. He saw a light go on in a window on the second floor. He could see Peg peeling off her coat. She had a blue sweater underneath, tight to accentuate her breasts.

She walked out of the frame, and then another window lit up, where she reappeared. He watched her move across the apartment through a series of squares like a cartoon strip.

Cartoon *strip* was apt. He could see that she was taking off her clothes. She was too drunk to care that someone could catch glimpses from the street.

Or maybe alcohol had nothing to do with it. It was just the way she was.

When she reached the last panel of the cartoon, the bedroom no doubt, she was down to her bra and panties. She came close to the window, a perfect view, and then disappeared altogether as a shade came rolling down.

He moved away from the parked car and headed up her walkway. He entered the building's foyer.

The names on the buzzers included a P. Shore on the second floor.

He figured that must be Peg. She lived alone.

Dynamite.

He pressed the buzzer.

After a moment, she came on the intercom and said, "That was fast." She buzzed to unlock the door.

He stepped inside, closing the door firmly behind him.

As he walked up the stairs, one step at a time in steady thumps, he reached into his coat pocket. He pulled out the wool face mask. On the second floor, he slipped the mask over his head and positioned the holes over his eyes, nose and mouth. He stepped up to the door of her apartment.

He placed his thumb over the peek hole.

He used his other hand to knock.

"It's unlocked," she sang out to him. "Did you bring Sam with you?"

Pete buzzed the intercom in the building's foyer, cradling a brown sack containing the six-pack of Sam Adams in bottles, just as she had requested.

He had a hard-on pressing against his jeans.

Granted, Peg belonged to Kevin and Kevin was a friend. Pete and Kevin had known each other since the seventh grade. Their bonds ran deep, which made tonight all the more awkward, but damn it...

Peg was horny for him and she was deliciously hot, and it wasn't the first time in human history that a chick had fallen for her boyfriend's best friend. These things just sort of happened in life. You couldn't deny that.

And anyway, Kevin had only been seeing her for what—six weeks? And Kev was a good-looking guy, pumped with personality, who had no trouble moving on to the next appetizer on his plate. From his behavior tonight, it was entirely possible that Kevin wasn't even all that interested in Peg anymore. He had been scoping out all sorts of chicks at O'Dell's tonight, jamming Pete with his elbow and murmuring comments that Peg couldn't hear. Or maybe she could? *Check out that ass... Ooh, cleavage... Sweet legs...*

So Kevin would be okay with all this, wouldn't he? If not, Pete would chalk it up to a drunken misadventure. Blame the booze. Or blame Peg for coming on to him.

Hell, blame *Kevin* for bragging about Peg's exquisite blowjobs. A guy just can't dangle that kind of temptation, like teasing a hungry dog with a slab of steak. You just don't...

Kevin really did use the word "exquisite," too

When Peg's intercom failed to reply, Pete buzzed it a second time.

He imagined she was slipping into something slinky, getting the apartment ready, maybe lighting some candles. God, he couldn't wait to see those tits, round and perfect, as she lay back on the bed sheets...

Bzzzzzzt.

He grabbed for the door and caught it in mid-buzz. He entered the staircase and headed for the second floor. He moved up the stairs quickly, every second one second too many in the distance between now and devouring every inch of her body.

He knocked on her apartment door, then noticed it was already cracked open. He stepped inside.

"I got the beer," he said, shutting the door behind him.

He was met by silence.

The shades had been closed, the lights dimmed. He grinned. "Peg, where are you? Beers are cold. I guess I better check the bedroom..."

He took one step forward and then stopped upon hearing a strange, high-pitched noise. It sounded like a dog whimper. But Peg didn't have a dog.

He listened, then heard it again, coming from another part of the apartment. It wasn't exactly a sexy come-on noise or a greeting. What the hell was she doing?

"Peg, you okay?"

He placed the beers down on the sofa. He headed for her bedroom. She was already pretty drunk, maybe she had fallen and hurt herself?

"Peg—"

Pete rounded a corner and then shouted. Something horrific and bloody staggered toward him—a distortion of Peg—her eyes replaced by raw, red holes. Her jaw moved but she was unable to speak, emitting squeaks. A sharp red line stretched across her neck, oozing multiple streams of blood that soaked the upper half of a white nightgown.

"Holy fuck!" Pete stumbled backward, tripping over his own feet, and then he felt a solid blow to his back, followed by a fiery, piercing pain.

He spun around, swinging his fists at the source of the blow, but not close enough to make contact, flailing at air.

A man in a green ski mask faced him, two fierce eyes, lips parted, teeth bared like some kind of animal.

The pain spread fast. Pete reached back and felt the shaft of a knife jammed in his back. He stumbled madly, clawing for it, trying to get a firm grasp on the handle. He crashed into Peg and they became entangled, falling together to the floor.

The man in the ski mask came forward and retrieved the knife, pulling it out of Pete's back, and for a split second Pete was grateful, but then he knew there was nothing to be grateful about, absolutely nothing, because the blade was coming at him again—

It struck Pete in the chest.

Pete gasped for air. Blood filled his lungs. He pulled away from Peg, who thrashed on the floor, grabbing blindly at him as if he was the attacker, scratching at him with her fingernails, kicking with her feet.

Forcing back the exploding pain, pulling together every ounce of his strength, Pete plowed into his attacker. The attacker punched at him with his fist, striking Pete's face before falling off balance and crashing into a chair.

Pete kept going at him. The attacker shoved him away. The two men faced each other, panting heavily, arms outstretched, about equal in size—

However, there was nothing equal about this battle. The attacker had a knife. Pete knew he had to tackle this man and get the weapon away if he was going to survive the next few minutes. He was losing a lot of blood and his head filled with a swarm of bees…

Pete charged the attacker. The two men grabbed at each other, staggering around the room, landing and missing punches, until Pete felt the blade hit for the third time, the worst of the three, the most painful, and at that moment he envisioned faces, the people he would never see again, his parents and brothers. He filled his mind with them, a final image before darkness took over.

Sputtering on the floor, blood and strength draining fast, Pete curled up and squeezed his eyes shut, waiting for death, but the attacker had another plan. He grabbed Pete by the hair and lifted his face from the carpet.

Pete opened his eyes just in time to see the point of the blade.

———

One dead, one almost.

"Almost" remained on the floor in her red-white nightgown, moving around on all fours, blindly knocking into a chair, then heading in another direction, hitting a wall.

"Scream," he encouraged her.

She tried, but couldn't, gurgling in her own blood. He had captured her scream in his digital voice recorder before slashing her speechless.

"Lose something?" he asked. Then he said, "Wait. I found it." He pressed a button on the handheld device and played the scream back at her.

She scrambled toward the source of her voice.

He stepped away and she banged into a table.

Finally, she sat up against a wall, gasping.

He walked over and kneeled in front of her.

He took her hand. It was trembling. He uncurled her fingers and placed something in her palm.

"This is for you."

He wrapped her fingers around it.

"It's your eye."

If she could have screamed, she would have let out a whopper.

Within ten minutes, she was dead.

He pulled himself up on the couch. He pulled off the face mask. His face was wet with sweat. He rubbed it with his hands.

Two in one day. A double header. And he had paid for it.

His ankle hurt like hell from the little dance with Pete. It was probably sprained. It needed ice. He couldn't walk on it right now.

Just as well.

He reached into the paper bag on the sofa cushion next to him and took out one of the beers. He removed the cap, threw it on the floor and took a long sip.

He could stay here for a little bit. She lived alone. It would take about a day for people to get curious and come looking for her, and by then he'd be gone. If someone buzzed sooner, she had a back porch with steps leading into the alley. A getaway route.

He had time to regroup, clean up, and enjoy his trophies.

He touched the cold beer bottle to his ankle. He giggled through the pain.

Tonight had been fun. Maybe he wouldn't wait so long for the next one.

As he took another sip of beer, the telephone rang.

He paused. He lowered the bottle from his lips. He listened to her answering machine pick up.

"Hi, this is Peg. I'm not home or maybe I'm not in the mood to answer the phone right now. But if you leave a message, I'll probably call you back."

After a beep, a young man's slurred voice sounded in the speaker: "Hey, babe, it's Kev. You're probably passed out. I'm about to crash. Just wanted to say hey. I'll call you tomorrow night. Maybe we can go out again or something. Six-dollar pitchers at Dolly's. Okay. Anyway. See ya. Be good."

The call disconnected.

He thought to himself, *Come on over, Kev. The party's just getting started. There's room for one more.*

He leaned back on the sofa and drank another beer. He listened to the first entry in his scream collection.

He couldn't wait to add to it.

Chapter Twenty-Six

Ellen sat at a table in Kaffinate, only two blocks from her usual cafe, but coffee was coffee, and she just didn't want to run into Charles right now. In fact, it wouldn't bother her if she never set foot inside of Pacific Coast Coffee again. Sometimes it was best to start a new chapter.

And this place was okay, a bit retro-beatnik, with a pseudo art gallery on the walls and folksy acoustic guitar strumming through speakers. The publications were more interesting, including a pile of what appeared to be various homemade zines with poetry, drawings and rants.

In her heart, she knew that the relationship with Charles had become broken beyond repair. Things had already been delicate when Peg had swooped in and made them worse. Ellen wouldn't blame Charles if he never wanted to see her again.

She felt anger at Peg for trying to take Charles's notebook and then trying to push some other guy on her. She was sick of people who felt free to shove her around.

This morning, more than anything, she had wanted to drag Peg into the back room at the Book Shelf and give her an earful.

And no, her ire wasn't fueled by jealousy because Peg was pretty and outgoing, without a worry in the world.

Peg was just a loudmouth who got in the way of other people's lives.

Ellen realized that this was why she liked books so much. They sat silent in her big bookcase, politely offering their spines but otherwise remaining unobtrusive until she reached out and initiated the acquaintance. They didn't scream at you from across the room, not like

TV or movies or the radio. They remained closed until you lifted the cover, like opening a doorway, choosing to enter their world. You knew what to expect: words on paper that moved through your head at your own pace, your own volume, in your own space.

Not many people understood and appreciated this unique and special bond with the written word.

Charles did.

Ellen left Kaffinate and headed to work.

She arrived on time, looked around for Peg, didn't see her, and started unloading a cart of new arrivals in biographies.

After a while, Terri walked over to her.

"Do you know where Peg is?"

Ellen shook her head.

Terri checked her watch and sighed. "Well, this isn't the first time she's gone missing in action. I wish she was more responsible and reliable—like you. Ten to one, she's hung over in some boy's apartment."

Ellen had to nod in agreement, thinking back to how wasted Peg had sounded on the phone the night before—and it hadn't even been eight o'clock when she called from the bar.

"Do you have a minute?" Terri asked Ellen.

"Of course," said Ellen.

Karen walked past them, and Terri said quietly to Ellen, "Follow me. This is just for you, not for the others."

Ellen followed Terri into the back room, curious about what was to come.

They stood together just inside the doorway, surrounded by boxes of books and various promotional displays.

Terry said, "District is opening up a new store. It'll be downtown in the Loop, near State and Randolph."

"Yes, I heard about that."

"Out of all my girls—and one guy—you might be the quietest, but I also think you're the smartest. You've been with us for a while and it's obvious you know the business. You've been involved, in one way or another, with just about every aspect of this store. They're going to have an open position at the new store for an assistant manager. If you're interested, I would put in a wholehearted recommendation for you. Now, to be honest, I don't know how long you want to stay in this type of work. Lord knows we aren't seeing a booming business in this industry. That's why we keep adding all this other crap—the coffee and bagels, CDs and greeting cards. Fewer people bother to read anymore. They're too busy with their cable channels and video games and the Internet. But there are still enough book readers to keep us going and make all this worthwhile and even rewarding. I know how you love books—you're the best-read employee on my staff. If I can help, are you interested?"

At first, Ellen couldn't believe it. She couldn't imagine herself as an assistant manager, telling people what to do, helping to run an entire store. But Terri's vote of confidence filled her with a positive feeling that maybe she could really pull it off.

Ellen realized she wanted to stay in the book business. This wasn't a brief stop on the way to someplace else as the job was to many of her co-workers.

"I'm interested," said Ellen. "I'm flattered that you thought about me. I...I really think I could do it. I mean, I'd have a lot to learn."

"There's training involved."

"Thank you, Terri..."

Terri reached out and hugged her.

Ellen felt a sudden urge to cry, but held back. People didn't hug her very often. And she never initiated hugs. But this one felt good.

———

Shortly before noon, Terri said, "Well, I don't know whether to be worried sick or just more angry."

She stepped out from behind the cashier counter and approached Ellen and Karen at the bargain books table, where they were replacing "Two-for-$10" stickers with "Three-for-$12."

"I've called Peg all morning and there's no answer," said Terri. "You don't think she had her days mixed up and thought she had today off, do you? It's happened before. That girl can be such a flake."

After Terri left, Karen muttered, "She should just fire her. She's so unreliable."

Ellen said nothing. Her imagination had started to take her to dark places that she didn't want to discuss. What if Charles really was a schizophrenic killer? What if he had no control over his other half? What if he had gone after Peg?

The notion seemed ridiculous, but the entire past few weeks were surreal, so anything was possible.

She could just as easily imagine Peg moaning in bed with a puke bucket at her side. Peg had once bragged about her "puke bucket", as if it was a symbol of a true party girl.

Toward the end of her shift, Ellen walked over to the mystery-thriller section and scanned the end of the alphabet for Robert Walker. There were several Robert Walker books.

She found *See No Evil*, the book about a serial killer who removed the eyeballs of his victims…and the book that Peg had said she had sold to Charles.

Ellen flipped through the book until she found one of the murder scenes. She read a brief passage.

He reached for the curve of her eye, dried and unblinking, fingers digging into the rim of the socket, squeezing and plucking the object like a grape from a vine.

"Disgusting," Ellen said out loud, slapping the book shut.

Reading that was a mistake, she thought to herself.

Now she felt even more nerve-rattled.

She saw Karen walk past, trailing a customer, offering to help in a half-hearted tone. The customer shook her off.

"Karen," said Ellen.

Karen turned. Ellen walked over to her.

"What's the name of your friend in the police department? The detective?" asked Ellen.

"Jack Allen?" Karen said.

"Yeah. I was wondering…could you give me his phone number?"

"Sure. Why?"

"Well, there's this, um, really strange man in my building, and with these recent murders, I thought I'd tell him about this guy."

"A weird guy in the city of Chicago?" said Karen. "Gee, sounds like you've cracked the case."

Ellen forced a chuckle. "I know, they must get a lot of tips…"

"Hundreds."

"But this guy gets really weird mail sometimes and I just thought…"

"Sure, give him a call. Add your name to the list," said Karen. She led Ellen to the cash register counter and wrote out Jack Allen's name and phone number on the back of a flyer promoting an upcoming appearance by an author-chef.

Ellen took the flyer and thanked Karen. "No problem," said Karen.

Ellen wondered if she really had the courage to call the police on Charles and finger him as a suspect.

Best-case scenario: the police would look into it and find that her suspicions were ridiculous and impossible, just like their other one hundred leads. Then she would know for absolute sure.

But even under this best-case scenario, there would be bad consequences. If she was willing to call the police on Charles, it was a sure sign that their relationship was dead. He would never forgive her. And perhaps she would never find another man with whom she could bond so passionately. Sending the police after Charles was a major roll of the dice.

Could she do it anonymously?

She folded up the flyer and retreated to the back of the store to put it in her purse, which was stashed out of sight with her coat in an employee-only area of the back room.

As she opened her purse, she caught sight of another scribbled phone number—Seymour's phone number on a white napkin.

She recalled their encounter. She wished she had an excuse to call him. She felt so alone right now and Seymour was a true ally…a fellow war veteran. She remembered the way he had looked at her, surprised by her physical transformation.

She thought about the spelling bee certificate she still had in her possession and realized it was the perfect opening…

She went to the phone and dialed the number on the napkin. She vowed to hang up if the dour, narrow-faced blonde answered.

After six rings, Seymour said hello. But his voice was on an answering machine.

She forced herself to leave a message, which she promptly regretted when the words came out garbled and hesitant. "Seymour… Hey…it's Ellen… I'm… I have… never mind, I'll call back some other time."

She hung up.

And spat, *"Damn!"*

When nothing goes right, nothing goes right…

Evening arrived quickly, another day shortened by the winter.

"Peg never called," said Terri. "Now I'm really worried."

Karen said, "Well, nobody's found any fresh murder victims today."

Terri snapped, "Karen, don't be morbid."

Ellen put on her coat. "I'll stop by her apartment and see if she's home. She lives just a few blocks away." It would only take a minute and might yield a quick and simple explanation for her absence.

"Thank you," said Terri. "I know it's probably nothing, but it would be nice to rule out any trouble. And once you find that she's okay, tell her to get her butt in here tomorrow morning by eight o'clock sharp. One more no-show like this and she's going to be looking for new work. I'm serious this time."

The sky held a deep darkness, without stars, shrouding the residential streets in blacks and grays. Ellen entered Peg's apartment building, stepping out of the winter chill and into the warm foyer.

She found the buzzer for P. Shore and pressed it. She waited for Peg's voice to crackle on the intercom, even if all she said was "Go away."

Instead, Ellen was met with silence.

She buzzed again, longer and more aggressively.

After another wait, she buzzed for a third and final time—letting it continue for a good ten seconds. If that didn't bring Peg's head out of the puke bucket, then nothing would.

The ten-second buzz was followed by more silence.

She waited several minutes. Then she turned and left the building, pushing through the door that led back outside.

She walked to the sidewalk and then turned around, looking back at the building. She glanced upward, looking for Peg's apartment on the second floor.

At that moment, a shadow pulled away from one of the windows.

Ellen froze. Was it Peg? Ellen straightened up, looking for any further movement. She could see a dim light behind a row of drawn shades. Wasn't that Peg's apartment? Or was she farther to the left?

Ellen waited for the shadow to return.

She considered going back inside the building to buzz some more. Did Peg know it was her? Was it Peg in the window?

Ellen grew more unsettled. The shadow didn't return. Had Ellen seen anything at all? She decided to go home. Her next action would be to call Peg's phone and leave an urgent message for her to respond. And then what? She could always try to reach Peg's boyfriend, Kevin.

If Kevin was unreachable or didn't have answers, she had Detective Jack's phone number.

Ellen knew one thing for certain: she couldn't sit around and do nothing.

She headed down the street, stepping in and out of the sporadic reach of street lamps.

The air remained bitter cold, another Chicago deep freeze on its way. She didn't see many other people out and only the occasional car.

As she turned a corner to head up the street that led to her apartment, she heard a short scraping sound, like a shoe brushing across pavement. It was a small noise, not close, but amplified by the quiet.

Ellen stopped and turned.

She didn't see anyone. The sidewalk was empty. Then what had she heard?

Was somebody following her?

Ellen picked up her pace. She fought back a rise of panic. She told herself to be calm. Home was only a few minutes away.

He kept out of view, nestled in the shadows. He watched her enter her building. So frail. So vulnerable.

After a few minutes, he saw the lights snap on, illuminating the lower-level apartment. A future death scene.

He was determined to get inside to do his dirty work. *Where there's a will there's a way.*

He closed his eyes and killed her in his latest mind play.

He fantasized about her screams…

Chapter Twenty-Seven

E llen entered the vestibule of her building with the uncomfortable feeling that she was being watched. She continued to look behind her for any sign of unusual movement. She thought about Peg and calling Detective Jack. How long until Peg's absence was deemed suspicious? Of course, it was entirely possible that Peg was out with Kevin, maybe even getting loaded again. But there was also a madman loose in the neighborhood. Ellen planned to leave Peg an urgent message on her answering machine, something like "Peg, please call back. Just let us know if you're okay…"

And if that didn't generate a response, she'd call the police.

Ellen checked her mailbox—bills and credit card pitches. She took one final look around before producing her key and opening the door that separated the vestibule from the apartment units. She stepped inside and the door closed behind her. She heard the click of the latch and felt safe. The building's warmth surrounded her.

Ellen walked down a short corridor, bypassing the staircase leading upstairs to the nice units. She unlocked the door to her garden unit apartment. She stepped inside, flicking the light switch. She shut the door, a second barrier against the outside world. She flipped the bolt into place and hooked the chain for good measure.

Ellen stepped into her living room, turning on a lamp. She dropped her purse on the sofa. She placed the mail on her computer table. She walked across the room, drawing the shades. That was one negative about being at street level: you were in a fishbowl for everybody to see. Maybe she could get the building owner to plant some bushes in front of her windows? That would help.

Ellen checked her answering machine. Typically, it showed no life, but today there was a message waiting, blinking in red.

Peg?

Ellen hit *play*.

It was Charles.

He didn't sound good. Had he been drinking? His voice shook, nervous and uncertain. His tone sounded heavy, as if he'd been dragged underwater.

"Ellen, it's Charles. I know you're at work, but I wanted to leave you this message. I know things have been difficult. I—I want to apologize for walking out on you the other night. Everything was just...getting to me. I don't know, maybe you've moved on, and you have somebody else, but I'd really like to...talk. Just get together and talk. Everything feels unresolved right now. So...please. I need to see you. Even if it's for the last time. Anyway... I look forward to hearing from you. Thank you, Ellen. Goodbye."

Ellen stared at the answering machine, paralyzed by a rush of conflicting emotions.

Should she call him back?

His voice penetrated her skin and sent her blood racing. She couldn't stop the effect he had on her.

Damn it, I don't know what to do.

Ellen wished she had someplace to turn to, someone to talk to. Her emotions were badly confused. It was easier when she had no dates, no social life, just this apartment with its big bookcase of books.

Be careful what you ask for, because you might get it. It was an old cliché, but certainly apt.

Ellen followed through with her intentions to phone Peg. The answering machine picked up after five rings. Ellen told Peg to call her as soon as possible—if she didn't hear back soon, she would call the police.

Ellen headed into the kitchen. She searched the cabinets, but couldn't find anything appealing for dinner. She also didn't feel much like cooking tonight. More than anything, she needed a lazy meal. She pulled a menu for Argenti Pizza off the refrigerator, from beneath a butterfly magnet. She took it with her to the phone and ordered a sausage and onion, providing directions.

Then she crashed on the couch with a good book—a romantic epic of medieval Spain, loaded with history and melodrama.

After fifteen minutes, the door buzzer sounded.

Ellen jumped, startled from her reading. It couldn't be the pizza guy. They were never this fast. Then who?

Charles?

Ellen hurried to the intercom.

She pressed the small black button and asked, "Who is it?"

"Hi, this is Peg," came the familiar voice through the static.

Peg!

Ellen buzzed to let her in. *Thank God*, she thought. *All that stupid worrying for nothing.* Ellen's worrying was replaced by anger. She was going to have to warn Peg that she was flirting with getting fired by Terri. Maybe Peg didn't care.

In fact, what *did* Peg care about?

When the knock sounded at her front door, Ellen quickly unhooked the chain and flipped the bolt. She threw open the door, exclaiming, "Peg, we've been—"

But it wasn't Peg.

A tall figure in a green ski mask stood before Ellen.

Ellen gasped and started to slam the door on him. He burst forward. The force knocked Ellen backward. She stumbled and landed on her back.

The intruder pushed inside the apartment and shut the door behind him. He stood over her.

Ellen screamed.

He pounced on her before she could get back on her feet. Her head hit the floor and she saw stars.

"Please—" she begged. She struggled, but the attacker was heavy, pinning her down. Then she saw the knife blade. He brought the tip to her throat, touched the skin, and she stopped talking. She remained silent, except for her panting. *Please don't cut me.*

With his free hand, he reached into a coat pocket for something. Ellen stared into his eyes, isolated by the ski mask. They were dark brown.

Was it Charles? Or *Darren*?

Keeping the knife tip at her throat, the attacker produced a thin, rectangular device. It was a handheld recorder, the type used by busy executives to dictate letters or capture ideas.

He pressed a button with his thumb.

He held the device to Ellen's ear for her to listen.

She heard, "Hi, this is Peg. I'm not home or maybe I'm not in the mood to answer the phone…"

It was Peg's answering machine. He had recorded the greeting off her machine and played the beginning over the intercom.

The intruder clicked another button to play a second recording. He shoved the device against Ellen's ear.

Ellen was forced to listen to Peg's long, agonized scream. It ended with sputtering and choking.

Ellen saw the mouth in the ski mask smile.

She said, "Please don't—" and the attacker's eyes grew wide and the blade pressed harder against her throat—not quite puncturing the skin—and she clamped her mouth shut.

The intruder brought the recording device in front of his face and worked the buttons with one hand, while keeping the blade at her throat.

Ellen realized in an instant: *Oh my God he's going to record me as he cuts my throat.*

She squirmed but had no place to go.

Ellen's left arm brushed something on the floor.

It felt like rubber.

It was her boot.

Please, God, let it be the one…

She grasped at it, fingers scratching, straining to reach inside…

The intruder brought the recorder toward Ellen's mouth. He removed the knife from her neck and raised the blade to one side, positioned to slash her throat.

"Scream," he said. He pressed the *record* button.

Ellen swung the hammer against the intruder's skull with every ounce of strength in her. It made a sickening, piercing *crack*. The intruder's head jerked to one side. He dropped the knife and recorder.

Ellen struck him again, smashing the hammer into his cheekbone, and the intruder roared, stumbling away on his knees. This allowed her to sit up and strike again with even more force, this time hammering into his forehead, producing another ugly *crack!*

She saw splotches of red appearing under the ski mask. He tried to get to his feet while holding out his hands, a desperate shield, and she swung the hammer at him again, going right between the hands and into his face, into his upper jaw, shattering teeth. She felt the impact vibrate up her arm and into her shoulder...

The intruder dropped to the ground.

He became very still.

Blood flowed from the center of the ski mask, out of both nostrils.

Ellen felt tears filling her eyes—blurring her vision—and she forced them back. *Stop! Don't lose it now.*

She gripped the hammer tight. If he moved a muscle, she would strike again...

He didn't move.

Was he dead?

His eyes were shut. One had swollen badly, an egg lifting out of the ski mask. The skin around it was turning dark colors.

Was it Charles?

She had to know. The possibility was driving her mad. The answer was finally in front of her. Her heart pounded and anxiety seized her ribs until they ached. She reached down and took hold of the bottom of the ski mask...

She started to peel upward. She lifted the mask off his chin. The fabric was wet and spongy from the blood. She brought it up over his mouth, a red hole of broken, jagged teeth. She continued lifting the face mask.

One eye opened.

His hand shot out and grabbed her wrist. She screamed and dropped the hammer. He pushed her away.

Ellen scrambled backward on her hands and feet.

The intruder sat up, looking from side to side with his one eye, searching frantically…

The knife.

Ellen saw it on the carpet, about four feet away.

She lunged for it.

The intruder jumped on her, pounding her with punches to slow her down. She continued to strain for the knife, her arm outstretched…

But he got to it first. He thrust the blade at her as she leapt away from him…

The blade struck her thigh and sunk into the flesh.

Ellen collapsed, screaming. The pain exploded in her leg and up her spine. She had never felt anything like it before. It was as if somebody had injected fire into her body.

The attacker grabbed the knife handle and pulled the blade out of her leg. Ellen surged forward, hobbling across the living room, lopsided. She heard him grunting, crashing past furniture, in close pursuit.

Ellen staggered out of the living room and into the corridor that led to the rest of her apartment.

She jumped inside the only room that had a lock. The bathroom. She slammed the door shut just in time, as the attacker's body crashed against the wood.

He pounded with a fist. She saw the door vibrate against the frame.

It would only be a matter of time before he burst through.

She was trapped. The bathroom had no window. She had no weapons. Or did she…?

Ellen searched the bathroom frantically. There had to be something to defend herself with…

The pounding on the door stopped.

Ellen froze and listened. She leaned against the sink, taking weight off her injured leg. It dripped coin-sized spots of blood on the tile floor.

She heard footsteps walking away from the bathroom door.

Surely he hadn't given up? Ellen gripped the cut on her thigh. Blood seeped through her fingers. She felt dizzy, but commanded herself, *Don't faint*.

Then she heard the footsteps return.

She held her breath.

An enormous *POW* struck the other side of the door, near the handle.

She realized, *He's using the hammer.*

After a moment, there was a second *POW*.

Maybe it would take two minutes, or maybe ten minutes, but he was going to get inside the bathroom and kill her.

POW.

Ellen searched the cabinets for something to defend herself with. What could she use? The tiny razor she used to shave her legs? Her hair dryer?

POW. The wood began splintering on Ellen's side of the door.

Just before the next *POW*, Ellen heard a buzzing. It took her concentration away from searching the cabinets.

Someone was pressing her front door buzzer. The pizza guy? Or maybe someone had heard the noise and they were checking on her?

It didn't matter—whoever it was, she had to get to them.

Ellen pictured the intercom by her front door. The little round speaker. The black buttons.

Could she get past her attacker to reach the button—just for a couple of seconds—to scream for help over the intercom and lean on the buzzer to get them inside? It was her only chance at survival.

POW. The hammer stuck the door again, followed by the *bzzzz* of the front entryway intercom. It had to be the pizza guy. Thank God for his persistence.

But he wouldn't buzz forever.

If she waited too long, he might leave. She had to act fast. She had to strike first against her attacker and get past him…

In the medicine cabinet, she found a small book of matches, which she used to light candles in the bathroom, sometimes during a late night bubble bath with a romance novel.

The matches excited her for a moment, until she realized they weren't a very good defense, just a tiny flame. Unless…

The attacker struck the bathroom door again with a forceful *POW* that splintered more wood.

Ellen figured that each slam of the hammer put the intruder off balance for at least a few seconds before he wound up for the next strike. If she timed it just right…

POW.

Immediately after the hammer struck, Ellen threw open the door.

The attacker had started to pull the hammer back, and his stumble indicated he was truly startled to see his victim open the door for him.

Ellen held a flaming book of matches in one hand. She sprayed an aerosol can of hairspray with the other.

She aimed for his one open eye.

The flammable spray created a blowtorch. A whoosh of flames shot forward into his face, igniting the wool ski mask.

The intruder screamed as his face burned. Ellen dropped the matches and aerosol can and ran past him. He spun in a circular dance, slamming his hands against the scorched portion of his mask.

Ellen ran for the intercom, limping badly, her left leg throbbing.

"HELP ME!" she screamed.

The attacker charged after her.

Ellen threw herself against the intercom, pressing the buttons. "HELP ME HELP ME HELP ME!"

She continued screaming and buzzing until the intruder grabbed her. He had lost some of his strength and coordination, but remained ferocious and relentless.

She pulled away from his grasp with nowhere to go but back into the living room. She ran several steps and then her bad leg gave way. She tumbled hard to the floor.

The intruder advanced toward her. His wool mask, bloody and scorched, seemed to fuse into his features, creating a horrific, creature-like face. He approached Ellen as she lay on the ground, flat on her back. He held the knife in a white-knuckled grasp. He stood over her, planting a foot on either side of her.

He swayed, dizzy and sluggish from the hammer blows and burns to his face. He reached into his coat pocket. He brought out a small, clear plastic bag containing two round objects. It took Ellen a moment to realize they were two eyes that had been torn from someone's face. It took Ellen another moment to realize they were blue, and then she knew that they were Peg's.

"I don't have any gray," he said, looking into Ellen's eyes. He chuckled, twirling the knife blade in front of her face.

Ellen said, "Go fuck yourself."

She shot her fist forward into his groin, a solid hit to the testicles, the first and only punch she had ever thrown in her entire life.

The intruder roared, staggered backward, doubled up and dropped to his knees. He kept the grip on his knife.

Ellen tried to get up and run, but her left leg had gone numb and useless.

The intruder lunged at her, grabbing the ankle of her bad leg. He slashed with the blade, missing by inches.

He pulled on her leg. She fell with a gasp, landing next to him. As they rolled together on the ground, she kicked and punched to keep him away. He grabbed at her face, catching a fistful of hair, which he tore from her scalp. He sliced the blade at her, cutting her side, delivering new shockwaves of pain.

Ellen scrambled away from him, escaping another thrust of the knife. She fell against her enormous bookcase.

The killer crawled toward her. Ellen gripped the side of the bookcase with both hands. She pulled on it with all her strength. She shouted out loud, a primal roar, every muscle in her body straining to move the towering shelves.

The seven-foot tall, eight-foot wide bookcase creaked off balance and then gave way to gravity, pitching forward. She leaped out of its path. It landed on the intruder with an enormous crash that shook the apartment and rattled the windows like a thunderstorm.

The bookcase and its avalanche of books pinned him to the floor on his back. Only his head and one arm emerged. The arm still gripped the knife.

He wheezed and sputtered and made ugly noises from deep inside his shattered ribcage.

"Drop the knife," said Ellen.

The intruder exploded into a howl of psychotic rage, shouting everything in one long, extended rant of hate and vulgarity.

Ellen seized the hammer and brought it over.

"Let go of the knife," she demanded. When the psychotic man did not obey and bombarded her with more verbal abuse, she smashed his knuckles.

He howled but held on tight.

She continued to hammer his fist until the knuckles became raw lumps covered in blood, the bones shattering into more pieces with every blow.

He would not let go, and he continued to scream every horrid, insulting word he could utter, spouting profanity in rapid fire from deep in his gut, like a machine gun spraying venom, and it filled her with the pain and fury of a thousand rancid memories. Wearing the mask, lacking identity, he represented every man who had ever abused her.

Ellen raised the hammer and aimed for his skull. She prepared for one final blow with all of her strength to put out his lights forever.

She lifted the head of the hammer high into the air…

A hand grabbed her wrist.

She turned with a shout.

It was Charles. His chest was heaving, his face was red. She realized he had just broken through her door. Charles had been the person buzzing in the entryway.

"Charles…" she said, and her fingers loosened around the handle.

Charles took the hammer from Ellen. He lowered it to the ground.

"Don't do it," he said. "You'll kill him."

She looked at Charles. Then she turned back to her attacker.

She bent over him. She reached toward his face.

"Ellen—" said Charles.

Ellen began peeling off the ski mask. It stuck to the skin of his face, fused there by the flames. She tugged harder, ripping it free, exposing raw flesh. She lifted the fabric over the top of his head. She had to see…

Ellen gasped.

She stared into a familiar face.

"Ellen, do you know him?" said Charles, watching her reaction.

She took several steps back. She nodded and burst into tears. It was Seymour. Her fellow war veteran. George Ravenwood may have damaged Ellen…but he had destroyed his son.

Seymour turned his bloody, disfigured face away from her.

"Put it back on…" he mumbled, the psychotic rage evaporated, replaced by a thin, scared little boy's voice. "Please…put it back on."

"Who is he?" said Charles.

Ellen couldn't speak Seymour's name out loud. He wasn't that person anymore. He had been replaced by something poisoned and deranged.

She said, "Call the police. Tell them we have the killer."

Within ten minutes, sirens screamed and lights flashed outside every window of her apartment.

Chapter Twenty-Eight

The police interviewed Ellen the following day at the Lakeview station. Bandaged, healing and still very sore, she sat in a hardwood chair in a small, blank room and told them everything she knew about Seymour Ravenwood. She talked about his father's abusive behavior, the escape to Chicago together, and the recent reunion at the Book Shelf's café.

She described how perfectly normal he appeared then, seated with a pretty blonde companion.

Detective Jack Allen took particular interest in the blonde girl. "Did you catch her name?"

"I think it was Nikki."

The detective sighed and looked over at his partner, Officer Noel.

"What is it?" Ellen asked, catching their worried expressions.

Noel produced a snapshot of Nikki, a picture that appeared to have come from a family holiday gathering. "Is this her?"

Ellen nodded. Then her stomach turned. "Oh no...what happened?"

"Same as the others," said Allen.

Ellen knew what that meant. Murdered. Eyes removed. She wanted to vomit.

Allen reported, "He met her in a bar. Flirted with her for a few days. Gained her trust. Played the part of a regular guy. Then took her out late one night for a walk in the park..."

"Enough," she said. "I don't want to hear any more."

She answered questions about Peg next. The most agonizing moment of the day came when they played Peg's recorded screams and asked her to confirm the source.

"Yes. It's Peg. Please shut it off."

She needed a break. The constant questioning and small space were suffocating her.

"Can I see my boyfriend now?" she asked.

Charles was waiting for her in another part of the station. He had not left her side since bursting into her apartment. He had gone with her to the hospital, stayed overnight with her, and accompanied her to the police station.

The officers looked at one another. She saw a nod of agreement.

"We can resume this afternoon," said Detective Allen.

―――――

Ellen's mother arrived at the station later that day. She looked a mess. She wore mismatched clothes and no makeup. Ellen imagined her getting dressed in a panic and speeding to Chicago as fast as possible in her little Honda.

Ellen ran to her mother and hugged her. She told her mother that she loved her. It was the first time she had said that since childhood.

Ellen introduced her mother to Charles. Her mother eyed him warily.

"You better take good care of my girl," she told him.

"He is," said Ellen.

"I will," said Charles. "I promise."

"Good," said Ellen's mother. "Because she doesn't take no crap from nobody."

"Yes. I have seen that firsthand," said Charles, and he had to smile.

―――――

When the police arrived at the Decatur, Illinois home of George Ravenwood to talk to him about his son, no one answered the repeated ringing of the bell and knocking on the door. Calls to his phone remained unanswered.

Officer Bill Roberts circled the side of the house, looking through the windows for any sign of activity. As he stepped onto the rear patio, he noticed the back door was partially open.

That's when the wall of stench hit…

George Ravenwood was discovered in his bed. He had been stabbed to death. The blood had drained out of him, outlining his body in dark crimson.

His eyes had not been removed. They remained wide open and glassy. In this instance, the attacker had not wished to be anonymous.

Chapter Twenty-Nine

He showed up behind the glass door, leaned forward, a hand shading his eyes to peer into the darkness.

She saw him but he could not see her, and she held the moment to stare at him and admire his handsomeness all over again.

Charles tapped lightly on the glass and Ellen stepped out of the shadows. He smiled when he saw her. He held a small cardboard tray with two cups of coffee from Pacific Coast Coffee.

Ellen unlocked the front entrance and let Charles into the Book Shelf's new State Street store in Chicago's Loop.

"Hello, Assistant Manager," said Charles. "Don't you have any lights?"

"If I get here early and I'm alone, I like to keep them off for a while," she said. "It's just me and the books, having a quiet moment, before the support staff gets here, and all the customers and noise."

"You're weird," said Charles. "And I identify with you all the way."

She took the tray of coffees from him and set it aside. "You better not stay too long," she said. "You don't want to be late for Terri. Not in your first week."

"I'll go in a few minutes," he said. "But first, I have something for you." Charles pulled out a paper bag that had been tucked under his arm.

"It's a present," he told Ellen. "It's something I've been working on for several weeks. I was going to give it to you sooner, but things have been pretty crazy. I wanted all the commotion to die down. I wanted a time for us to be alone."

"That hasn't been easy," she said, sympathetic. After the Lakeview killer had been apprehended in her apartment, she had been thrust into the media spotlight—a jarring experience for a shy woman who had spent a lifetime avoiding attention. She never wanted to see another TV news camera again.

"This is for you," said Charles. He reached into the sack and took out his green notebook.

Ellen stared at the green notebook for a moment, startled. "Are you sure?"

"I'm sure. Take it."

She accepted it from him.

Charles said, "There's a reason I've been so secretive about my new notebook. I didn't want anyone to see it, not even you, until it was finished. It's a departure from anything else I've ever done. Open it to the first page."

She lifted the cover and looked inside.

The first page said: *For Ellen With All of My Love, Charles.*

"I've been writing for you," he said. "I don't know if it's any good, but it's from the heart. It's about us and how I feel about you. I might not be good about expressing these things to you out loud, when we talk, but I tried to capture them on paper. This is nothing like my other notebook. I was in an angry place and I was getting rid of demons. *This* is closer to who I really am."

She turned the page and read the first few lines of the opening entry.

"My life changed forever the day I met Ellen, a young woman of uncommon grace, warmth and beauty. My heart healed, my head cleared and I embraced the world again. She brought me into a brand-new space without boundaries, where strength and wisdom are driven by the essential goodness of the human spirit."

Ellen's eyes watered. She shut them before a tear could roll down her cheek.

She heard Charles chatting nervously, telling her, "I know it's not very subtle or sophisticated. It's probably not as good as the writing you like to read, or as good as any of the books in this store, but it's honest about how I feel. I just wanted to go with it, write it all down and see what happens."

She put down the journal and kissed him. Then she hugged him, holding him tight. He returned the embrace, and she felt the warmth of his body.

Ellen and Charles stood in each other's arms for several minutes, wordless among the thousands of books. They didn't need to speak and they didn't want to part, engaged in the slowest dance of all, the beating of two hearts.

About the Author

Brian Pinkerton is a USA Today Bestselling Author of fiction in the suspense, thriller, mystery and horror genres. His novels include *Abducted, Vengeance, Killer's Diary, Rough Cut, Bender, Anatomy of Evil, How I Started the Apocalypse, The Intruders, Time Warp,* and *The Gemini Experiment.* Select titles have also been released as audio books and in foreign languages.

Brian's short stories have appeared in anthologies including *Chicago Blues, PULP!,* and *Zombie Zoology.* His screenplays have finished in the top 100 of Project Greenlight and top two percent of the Nicholl Fellowship of the Academy of Motion Picture Arts and Sciences. Brian received his B.A. from the University of Iowa and Master's Degree from Northwestern University.

Curious about other Crossroad Press books? Stop by our website:
http://crossroadpress.com
We offer quality writing
in digital, audio, and print formats.

Subscribe to our newsletter on the website homepage and receive a
free eBook.

www.ingramcontent.com/pod-product-compliance
Lightning Source LLC
Chambersburg PA
CBHW030312200626
46816CB00002BA/867